The actual adventures of michael Missing

The Actual adventures of michael Missing

STORIES BY

Michael Hickins

Alfred A. Knopf   New York 1991

THIS IS A BORZOI BOOK
PUBLISHED BY ALFRED A. KNOPF, INC.

Copyright © 1991 by Michael Hickins

Certain of these stories were originally published in *The Quarterly*.

Library of Congress Cataloging-in-Publication Data

Hickins, Michael.
    The actual adventures of Michael Missing : stories / by Michael
Hickins.
      p. cm.
    ISBN 0-394-58741-3
    I. Title.
    PS3558.I229A64   1991
    813'.54—dc20   90-44011
                                                  CIP

Manufactured in the United States of America

First Edition

To Mom, Alfred, Charlotte Deluxe,

Michael Granville, C. M. A. Tomei-Hickins,

and especially to Michael R. Isby

contents

The actual adventures of michael Missing

a Person with a Gun is DAngerous to those Around him

I'm nineteen, I'm married, I have one kid, and I can't stand any of it. Someone will probably think I'm not diplomatic enough, but I've had it with talk that disguises the real item: anger.

How many times do we have to see the same things? Spanish couples in the subway letting their kids put dirty toys in their mouths because there doesn't seem to be a legitimate alternative, beggars with nothing but a bag of clothes and a battery-operated TV. Just for the record, while I was on my way to the R train at Eighth Street, on the uptown side, I gave the whole system one more chance.

A white guy about as thin as two fists asked me for forty-five goddamn cents when I passed him by the token booth. He was wearing a white T-shirt and had the word *Death* tattooed on his arm. I thought about it, and gave it to him. I mean, maybe just this one time someone isn't simply getting away with whatever they can until they or I die. As stupid as it was, I gave this guy the responsibility too, the awful, unfair onus of redeeming the planet, the whole fucking city. You can take so much sadness and then you have to do something angry.

I was on my way to see Orel, my old pal at Americans for a Leftist America. We used to work together back when I believed firmly but moderately in freedom and equality for all; I'd just quit three weeks ago.

The first time I saw Orel he was ripping off the phone company with a tape recording that reproduced the exact pitch of money being dropped into a pay phone. He got kicks institution-busting. I knew he'd get me the Florida driver's license I needed as long as I didn't tell him what it was for.

The bum at Eighth Street said, "God bless," and then, "Now I'm three-quarters of the way home—to Paris. Ha ha."

I was a chump again, because I'd given in to the old trust. The comforting lie that, if you wait and negotiate, the world will get better. Values that no longer apply.

"Gonna get a gun permit or something?" Orel laughed.

You got that one right, buddy, I thought.

I laughed too. It was a bad laugh, the laugh of someone bent on destroying family and self, but Orel didn't catch that. He was already halfway to his next self-congratulatory thought. We walked past the dope dealers and brightly lit porn marquees and into a comic-book store that smelled of cat piss and old paper. I checked out back issues of *Captain Gorgon* while Orel took care of my business with some Frank behind a curtain.

Orel wanted to have lunch, but I said I was busy. "Yo, later," I said. I learned that in Corona, where I spent six months trying to organize Spanish-speaking illiterates around getting a new stop sign on Forty-third Avenue and Hampton Street. "Yo, later." Who can blame them? Intransigent political inertia on either side.

"Give us a call, man. Keep in touch," Orel said. Not wanting to lose one of the flock. I hated that brotherly hopeful Us. I could spit on the people if I could just get them to stand still for a minute.

I called Alice, went to Florida, and came back. I had a

Colt and two hundred rounds of ammunition. Just for target practice.

We left Suzy and enough powdered baby junk to last a week with Alice's sister. Alice had her feet up on the windshield and a cup of Dunkin Donuts coffee in one of those cupholders that stick to the dashboard. As long as the car didn't stall, she seemed willing to enjoy the trip.

"Can we stop in Woodstock for some more tapes?" she asked girlishly. I fought back the impulse to bang my hand on the wheel. She couldn't be happy exactly, but she could be content when she was frittering away our money. I fought back the anger that always came over me then, and that had been at least 36 percent responsible for the miseries of our marriage, because I knew this was our last trip together.

"Sure." I grinned. She grinned back. For this smile, I'd fallen in love.

"Tell me again," she said, sensing my thoughts and maybe wanting to prolong that feeling. That feeling I was faking.

"We met at the prom. In 1979. I saw you dancing, and when your date went to get . . . punch, I think . . . I walked over to you. You told me you wouldn't—"

"No, I told you I couldn't," she interrupted.

"I'm telling this story. You said you couldn't. Okay. Your date went home; and we left later and walked to the Staten Island Ferry. We stayed on for like three hours and we had our first kiss with the spray from the East River in our faces."

"How did we kiss?" she asked.

"I was standing behind you, and I put my hand on your bare shoulder. You turned your head and I caught your lips as they passed. I let my hand touch your neck and your collarbone."

It was a lie, all of it, but she loved it. It was a good start for the trip.

"Now tell me where we're going again," she said.

"To some hippie friends of Orel's. They live in some electrified cabin upstate. Very rustic. They grow their own organic stuff."

"And they invited us?"

"Sure," I said.

I lied, of course. She nodded skeptically. Smart girl.

She smiled and nodded out. Sometimes it pissed me off that she slept through most of our drives, because they could be so pleasant. Since we weren't doing anything, there was a decent chance of having a good time together. But it gave me time to think.

I'd read about this couple living in Gilboa, New York, who was getting harassed because they didn't let hunters on their land. Shot at. Village thugs and out-of-town hunters were doing lovely things like shooting out their windows or pulling their veggies up by the roots.

I figured the best thing to do was go up there and shoot at people; the hippies might not agree once they caught on, but they weren't going to be in a position to argue.

People would get the idea pretty quickly, and lose their nasty recently acquired habits. I hadn't thought about bringing Alice along; I just did. Maybe I brought Alice along for revenge. Or as a test, which if it was a test, I don't think she had a chance of passing. She did have one chance: nothing can turn the world on its head like a Colt. It's got seven shots to a clip. It was the gun that brought the serf up to the level of the lord.

Alice sniffed snoozily when I asked her for change at the tollbooth. "Damn it, make yourself useful," I snapped. She started, and then her usual expression of indifference was back. The one she'd replaced earlier with a girlish grin. God, I hated the whole thing, shifting from one face to another for the rest of your life, supposedly.

It was November of 1980. We stopped in a chain restaurant in a small town that passes for a city in upstate New York. In the bathroom a guy was looking at himself in the mirror, girding himself. He was a washed-up forty, heavy and a little dandruffy. He inhaled audibly and said, "Oh boy." It was that bad out there.

There was a family of six at a booth in my line of sight. A cute little girl was creating a lot of attention for herself, mostly by torturing her brother, who seemed about five or six. The grandparent types were in their early fifties, and if there had been any justice, they would have been the parents. They watched the kids with expressions thin as their coffees.

The real parents were young. The mother used to be slim, and maybe attractive to her husband once. The father was young and still muscular, though you knew that wasn't going to hold for long. Neither could seem to stand watching their kids, and I couldn't blame them. As I said, God should have given them to the grandparents.

I also had the feeling the two parents still had some pure love for each other. I looked at Alice out of the corner of my eye. All we had left was what we used to enjoy together, like certain records and one-liners from movies. I could make her laugh, but it was all wrong the way we went about it.

The little girl was torturing her little brother. Suzy was also a little girl, and it bothered me that the little girl was torturing her father, indirectly at least, as much as she was torturing her brother. But what made me really furious was that her parents were young. Saddled with that kid, their lives were over for all real purposes. That man staring into his dish of cold french fries. Some weekend lunch. I pitied him and me and the inevitable cycle of our lives.

I pushed Alice out and into our 1971 Buick. But it wasn't over for me. I reached into the glove compartment and pulled out the Colt. Alice raised an eyebrow but didn't say anything. She wouldn't give me the advantage of asking what the hell that was doing there. I put it into my jacket pocket and closed the door. "Just wait," I said.

I walked to their booth and stopped directly across the table from the little girl. Her straight teeth were white, small, cute. She looked at me, and so did her parents and grandparents. They might have been used to such admiration from a total stranger. Then I leveled the Colt at her head.

"Buddy," I said to the father out of the corner of my eye, "I'm gonna take some of the misery out of your life."

The grandparents didn't blink. Maybe they were used to this too. Change the channel, only I'm not a TV and I'm going to blow this little girl's brains right out.

"Jesus," the guy said, not moving. The young mother gasped and grabbed her husband's arm.

"Mister, please don't do it," he said. "Whatever you want. Kill me instead. Don't hurt her. Kill me instead. Take anything, but don't kill my little girl."

"Don't get hysterical, and think about what you're saying," I said angrily. This guy made me want to throw up. Probably a bit of rehearsed heroism he dreamed up years before he had any kids to save, only he meant it, the sap. Wasn't he going to leave me any choice? He just kept asking.

"You miserable idiot," I said.

"Please, mister."

"I'd be doing you a favor, but you just don't get it. You're so hopeless I should kill you instead. Forget the whole thing," I said, irritated beyond belief. "Just never mind.

"Just drop it," I said, and walked out to the car.

"No gunshots?" Alice asked.

"Get that smirk off your face," I said. Out on the highway there were no more incidents or police. That was irrational, I told myself. That was illogical anger. The purpose I was really setting out for was fueled by rational anger. Rational anger. Justifiable rage. Intellectual. I'd better cut that other stuff out, or I'll never get what I want done, I thought.

"People won't let you help them," I said to Alice. She

laughed, damn her. She laughed. I knew I'd have to be careful with the hippies, or they wouldn't let me help either.

Alice dropped off to sleep again, and I don't think she was all that tired. I guess people sleep a lot when they're trying to escape something or someone. Alice was right to hate me. I wasn't even sleeping with her most nights anymore. Mostly I've been in self-imposed exile in the other room, while she and Suzy share the bedroom.

One morning last week she came into my room and sat on my bed. She whispered my name and ran her feather-shaped nails along the curve of my leg. I pretended I was still asleep. She wanted me to pull her to me and make love to her. I can still force myself to remember how hard I used to love her, but it makes me cry. I tried to push my face farther into the pillow and thought of strictly nothing.

I left Alice in the car when I went out to meet them. Ellen and Jerry Higgins in flesh and blood. Considering everything, they didn't have any business being so friendly. Gosh-happy hippie hello complete with soul handshake. What a bunch of longhairs, I thought.

I liked Ellen quite a bit, probably because Jerry was so damn passive. I shook her hand firmly; despite the overalls, she was pretty. Jerry leaned his hand on a tree while I talked. They didn't look stupid, just happy.

They were convinced that sooner or later people were going to stop taking potshots at them and theirs. I knew better, and I was going to make it my business that they were left alone sooner than later.

I introduced myself and said I was a friend of Orel's. I'd sort of forgotten the story was a lie, but they welcomed us anyhow. That figured.

Alice was still too obstinate to give me satisfaction, but she must have been surprised. She'd been looking at motels along the way, since it was obvious as hell to her that we weren't spending even one night in this legendary two-room house I'd described. I don't know what she thought was going through my mind.

At dinner I opened: "Orel told me about the trouble you folks been having." Orel, someone no one knew anymore, was a magical force, a point of reference.

"Yeah," Jerry said. "We hope that's over now, though."

"Or that it will be soon," Ellen said. "It's kind of a drag and I'm getting a little fed up."

"Maybe as long as we're here we can give you a hand," I said.

"We'll just wait it out like we've been doing," Jerry said evenly. It crossed my mind that he was beginning to suspect something. He hadn't seen the gun yet, and the ad wasn't coming out until the morning. I had to work on Ellen before he figured me out, but that wouldn't be too hard. I looked into her hippie-love blue eyes. Women are quicker to fight.

"Sometimes, you know, when people get together, they're, you know, stronger," I said. Feigning inarticulateness has the effect of making me seem sincere. Ellen leaned forward and said, "That's right on."

Alice thought I was flirting and kicked me under the table. This was a good sign, if Ellen thought so too. I was ready to use any weapons at my disposal.

These were not political hippies. They were anarchist agrarian hippies, God help them. I walked around the main room to see what if anything they were into reading, but all I found eventually were local newspapers on the floor of the outhouse (no plumbing).

Around the wood-burning stove, I got into my raconteur mood. Alice was bored and let me know, but fuck her. It was my vacation too, damn it.

"I used to work with Orel at the ALA," I said. Orel again. "My first mission was to organize Corona. The trick, and you've got to use a trick, is to get them united around a small issue, but one they care about. The idea is that they might win a small battle, say, for a stop sign or more police protection. Then, when they see what being organized can do, get them to take on a bigger issue. Develop leadership from within the community. Then Captain Marvel flies to the next trouble spot." I snorted and then laughed uncontrollably. I even caught Alice by surprise. I never told her why I quit working for the ALA.

"We called it social change. Naturally you assumed the change was for the better. You never said, 'We're providing a safety valve so these people don't get mad and simply take what's theirs.' And you assumed 'the people' is this heroic mass just waiting for a nice white Anglo to lead them to the quiet hum of city hall. That they were unhappy, frustrated, and looking for an outlet, an opportunity, a guy just like me. Me, in fact. I can even speak Spanish. But 'the people' was this bunch of Budweiser-addicted, fat, satisfied assholes who knew only one thing: white never means right. So who cared about a stop sign on Forty-third and Hampton Street? In the end, I quit because the money sucked or my friends hated my job, Alice might have divorced me or maybe I couldn't stand the hopelessness. And I couldn't stand that idiot Orel."

Alice looked at the floor again. Ellen and Jerry didn't know me well enough to know if I was kidding at all. Alice was right about one thing—telling her this was an act of love. We slept together that night; we got close without any wisecracks. It was the least sinister night we'd had since the baby was born. It was the first night I was sure I hadn't dreamed of killing either of them.

Jerry went to town after breakfast, and I knew I had to work quickly. But Ellen knew I'd come with a purpose, and she'd help me. She approved a little, just enough to give me room.

"What exactly do you want to do?" she asked. I liked the way she held her body. She was trying to corner me.

"Cause the momentum to shift. Put them on the defensive."

"How?" She smiled and looked down at the earth.

"Another person—a male person—just might do it."

She nodded, and without having been explicit I think I made her understand what I'd resort to if the occasion demanded. She wasn't going to give any more than tacit consent to violence, but I didn't need anything more yet. We were just outside the cabin. Alice walked out and, seeing us there, frowned.

I've never been able to stand slaphappy Scientologists, self-help enthusiasts, and guru-worship types, but Ellen's smile was a pure turn-on. Alice hated her sexiness.

I walked over to a tree at the other end of their farm and walked off fifty yards from that. The maximum effective range of the Colt. I missed a lot at first, but I got better as the morning went on. I did my best.

When Jerry came back, he was as mad as a hippie could be. "Man, is this your ad or what?" His hand was trembling as he held the *Gilboa Mountain Eagle* toward me. I took the paper. They'd done a nice job, and the ad was near the front of the sports section. It read:

> Tough guy with Colt will shoot ANYONE WHO comes to bother the Higginses or their property. Let no cowards CONFRONT the COLT.

"Sure," I said. I had the Colt at my side. Ellen and Jerry stood watching me, anxiously, I'd say. Alice wasn't around. Business as usual.

"We don't need this at all, man," Jerry said, his voice breaking.

"Nothing will happen," I said, "except that maybe some-one will try something nasty again, I'll point this lovely baby at them, and they'll go back, talk about it, exaggerate the size of the cannon, people will say I actually shot at them, and boom! problem solved."

Jerry looked at Ellen, and I took a step back, giving them a little room to exchange mute signals. Husband and wife, like so often, wife in charge.

"What are you practicing, then?" he asked. Maybe it was the last question he had permission to ask in that rude tone.

"Hey, I got to know how it works so no one gets hurt, right?"

You can look that one up in the NRA handbook.

I didn't see anyone else for the rest of the day. I'd shot more than half the ammo and I was deadly accurate within thirty yards.

Ellen came over to get me for dinner, and I looked into her eyes again. Maybe she wanted me and maybe she didn't. Maybe she simply wanted to use me so that people would leave her and her defenseless husband alone. I didn't care either way, but I took her hand. She smiled and wanted me to kiss her. I obliged her briefly.

"Interested in dinner?" she asked.

"Famished," I lied.

"Good. Tell me," she said as we walked, "why did you give up on your political work?"

Time for the import restrictions. You can't send world maps to India, calendars to Lebanon, denim material to Indonesia, CB radios to Northern Ireland, motorcycle helmets to New Zealand, horror comics and prison-made goods to the UK, any political literature to Belize (formerly British Honduras), or communistic material to Indonesia and South Korea.

When I finished the list, we'd been standing on the porch for almost a minute. Alice still thought I was trying to seduce

Ellen. She had it wrong. I knew I was simply a necessary evil in Ellen's eyes. If anything, my destroyed idealism was a turn-off.

Dinner went smoothly, I thought. At the table, no one spoke. Alice didn't deign to give me a look. She looked at Ellen, though, with scorn and a certain amount of pity. Jerry wanted nothing but to be rid of us, but hippie etiquette demanded that he tolerate us for a little while.

It got dark early, the way it does in the country with no lights to delay the night. We only had a few more hours to wait.

Alice came over to me on the rustic couch, which was wet with the humidity of an unwinterized cabin. That Alice would accept these conditions was striking enough.

"What you're doing doesn't make any sense," she said. I smiled coolly, smoothly.

She continued, "You've made your point, I'm sorry. You don't have to go through with anything. Nothing you've done is irrevocable. I know you're not an asshole."

How often did she think I was going to pull a stunt like this just to get her attention? It was really about making a difference in someone's life, for a change. And there was nothing about Alice or me worth reforming. If anything could have made me back off my plan, it was Ellen and Jerry. They seemed a little happy off on their own like this. But one thing was missing, something I could provide: peace.

A car pulled up the unpaved drive and headlights swerved through the windows.

"Hey," a loud young male voice called out. "Where's the Colt?" A rock came through the window.

Alice tugged at my sweater sleeve. Ellen and Jerry watched me go through the door. The guy was standing in front of the headlights now, pitching. Another at the wheel. I held the Colt at my side. "No hunting allowed," I said.

"Ha ha," he said.

I brought the gun up. Ha. The motor revved, the passenger door flew open from inside, the driver yelled, "Come on, get in."

This is rational, I thought. *Crack!* The car lurched backward, spinning in the gravel, and took off.

And now I was angrier than before. I felt relief and revulsion. I could see blood in the moonlight and a crater-sized hole where a nose should have been. It might have just been the shadows playing tricks, but it seemed his eye was pushed out by the impact and was dangling by a muscular thread. I felt fear.

Everyone was outside. Alice was holding her arms against her chest as if she were shot somewhere too. Ellen and Jerry stood apart from her; they were all thirty or so yards away.

I couldn't think of anything to say, although I wanted to very much. I would've said it was a very bad mistake.

I left Alice the car and beat it out of there. It took so long getting to Canada, it was safe to cross the border on foot. The farther north I get, the harder it is to take the cold. I ditched the gun in a river. Soon I'll freeze to death, thank God. I'm sickened by the sadness within me.

in tHe BOROughwidES

Sure, Ma. Whatever you say, Ma.

Nothing makes me more disgusted than a guy who's embarrassed by his mother. It happens all the time, so what's the big fucking deal? Anybody worth a shit is embarrassed by his mother.

Until my father died, it was the usual stuff—ill-timed hugs, badly dissembled crying jags.

After, she was worse. Dependent.

I used to really get a lot out of my dad's existence. There was a lot to learn. He wasn't a good man, but he was sincere. And he was fair, to strangers. He forgave them generously—because they were strangers.

After, all I did was suffer from his existence.

If my father still had eyes, I'd be a failure. Not for the classical reasons, but because I don't love my mother enough.

Every so often I call her, and she begs me to write. Like I was halfway across the world. I'm not even out of state.

About a year after he died, I was fourteen. She and I went to a movie in Manhattan. It was supposed to be educational for me because it was an old movie and she'd already seen it. It was the first time she went out of the house for anything. It took place in Paris, a small street, a gay little girl. Right away (the movie had hardly started) and my mother was jiggling around in her seat, poking me with her elbow, and telling me she grew up around there.

At the end of the movie, my mother stood up like we were alone in the house watching TV and she shouted, "No! No!" I led her down the aisle and stared at my feet, and I waited for her outside the bathroom. Educational as hell.

A few days later, I got mad at her for something entirely different, and I said, "He's been fucking dead now for over a year. Snap out of it already."

She ran into her room and locked the door. My father used to knock loudly and threaten to break down the door when she did that. I didn't do any such thing.

She was clearly going off the deep end. She came back out of her room wearing a lot of powder and lipstick all over her face, with a big clown smile drawn across half her snuffling mush.

"Is this what you want?" she asked me.

I wanted to jump out the window.

I also had this idea for winning the Nobel Prize by feeding all the starving people in India. I knew that if you got enough earthworms wriggling around, you could get a lot of fertilizer from it, and all of that stuff.

The annual science fair at school was coming up. I got this guy Dave to help me, because I needed someone who could stick things together and draw posters. He went along with the idea, because otherwise he would have had to do a solar house like four-fifths of the other kids.

Anyway, Dave's brother was adopted, and his name was Matthew. Matthew Beniac. As in maniac.

Matthew was a tough guy with a reputation. I once saw him pull off a minor theft in the candy store, and I didn't say a thing. So I was okay by him. But Beniac had been sent away to reform school, and he escaped from the Spofford Boys Correctional Facility the year of the worms and was zipping around Queens on an extremely tiny bike. It had no brakes, just sort of spun around until he forced it to stop. He had quit growing, except muscles. He carried a zip gun and a couple of knives that I saw personally one time, and people say he escaped from Spofford by beating up his shrink. Whatever.

No one wanted to see Matthew Beniac coming fast, crouched over the tiny bike, his little feet pounding the pedals, like someone had given him this worthless piece of shit for Christmas and he was going to wear it into the ground.

It was February, and I went out with Dave and this kid with a shovel to Flushing Meadow Park to dig for earthworms. The wind was blowing like it had a personal grudge against me. It took us an hour to fill six mason jars with worms and put the jars in shopping bags.

On our way back, we ran into a bunch of kids who were going to paint subway cars. We tried to get away, but they caught us, and this skinny Hungarian kid, ten feet shorter than me, put a knife to my throat.

And I didn't even live in a tough neighborhood. I guess it was the social climate.

"Whatcha got in the bags?" the kid wanted to know.

"Worms," I said.

"Fuck you," the kid said, pushing the blade in tighter to me.

"Look," I said.

But the kid didn't look. Instead, he punched me in the stomach.

I ask you, why did we have to just stand there and take it? But we did.

We had to.

My mother got herself into a hairy sweat when I got home

with Dave. She thought maybe we were dead from internal bleeding and wild animals were eating our corpses.

Sure, Ma. Whatever you say.

When the snow melted, Dave and me stopped working on the worms and went to play stickball in the park. The parkee was oiling the swings or doing some other useful thing. Dave started chalking in a new strike zone and I was getting fixed to test the rubber balls for bounce.

I said, "I hope some big kid doesn't ask for a swing."

There was always the danger that a big kid would ask you if he could take a swing. If you said no, then he would take the bat from you anyway. His friends were always watching, so when he missed, he kept trying until he hit the ball. Usually it took a dozen pitches, and the guy would get mad because they were too low or outside, and then finally he'd belt one over the bowling-alley roof.

You might as well climb up there from the start.

I had never had those or any other problems with Matthew Beniac, but when I saw him scooting across the park hunched over his bike, I knew in the pit of my testicles that that was all in the past. Beniac hopped off the bike before braking—it stopped out of blind obedience. "Come here, talk to me," he said in shorthand gangster talk.

"Sure thing," I said, with a song in my heart.

He was a quarter inch away from my face, if that.

"Does the name Canadreou mean something to you?" he said.

I said, "The name what?"

"Let me refreshen you," Beniac said, and he whopped me across the face with his open hand.

The blood rushed so fast, it was like my cheeks had split open. I put my hands up, but Beniac looked at me, and I put them back down. I was going to take it, and I was going to like taking it.

Whop. Whop.

I backed up slowly, trying not to cry.

My father hated it when I cried. "I'll give you a reason to cry," he used to say. Like he was going to break my knees. Because he had seen the war, and the world was a very serious place, and the people in it had real reasons to cry.

Beniac slapped and slapped.

"Fight back!" his brother Dave yelled. I realized there were people looking.

My back was up against the Cyclone fence, and I slid down to where Beniac had trouble slapping me.

"It's a good thing you didn't fight me," Beniac said, "or I would have killed you."

I started to cry, out of gratitude, because he could have but he didn't and he probably even had a right to.

I wanted to be his friend. I wanted to be like him, be dangerous. I wanted to hit people. To rob from the rich. Get killed.

At the water fountain, some fool gave me advice.

Yeah, yeah, I said.

At the science fair, the whole thing was a huge success. I won. But then I only got honorable mention in the boroughwides.

My mother wanted to sue. Whatever you say.

People said to me, "Great work. You sure learned a lot."

The hell with all that, I thought. What about my big idea? What about all the starving people in India? And I want to ask you, Why is the universe so stingy and short?

caPEr

On my fourteenth birthday Aunt Agnes came into my room and closed the door behind her. "Enjoy the party?" she asked, sitting with a delicate twitch of her ass on the edge of my bed.

"Sure," I said.

Years before, during the last hour of another party, the one celebrating her marriage to my Uncle Feldstein, I asked her what it was she did when she was "in the business."

She was sitting in an armchair, and I was cross-legged on our pale pink wall-to-wall carpet, trying to look up between her legs. My mother was standing apart at the other end of the room, and by that sense of mothers that all boys have, I knew that she was holding her breath.

"Well, Michael," Agnes said, stirring champagne with her finger, "gentlemen like yourself would call on me and we'd spend some time together. And then they'd pay me."

I was satisfied with that, my mother breathed again, and Agnes looked fresh with triumph.

The next day I told my friend Archie Winstin, "My uncle married a whore." I was proud of it, and I was proud of knowing it.

"That was great about the prize," my aunt said now, sitting next to me on my bed, in my room, which smelled of dirty socks and suddenly of drunkenness and perfume also. "Yeah, that sure was. That really was."

Agnes meant the prize I'd won for a picture I took of a man falling off a beam at a construction site. I was a creative youngster.

A lot of my pictures got published in the paper, so a prize wasn't a big deal to me then.

My aunt stood up and stripped herself; she was naked quickly. "Don't be afraid," she said, but at my age there was nothing else to do.

She got in bed next to me (stiff as an emery board) and smoothed my hairless chest and stomach. She began by kissing my shoulders.

I came all over my stomach.

Minutes later (I'm not showing off, I was fourteen), I was inside a woman for the first time. Fantasy already played a great role in my life. She was sitting on me and I had my eyes closed, seeing the lady in the stationery store where I stole in the hope of getting caught, and the skinny woman who worked in my uncle's Photo Lab and wore pink lipstick, and the teenage girl I had a crush on that my uncle used to go out with before he married Agnes. So maybe I was having my revenge.

I opened my eyes and stared at her breasts. "How can you carry those around?" I asked.

"You sort of get attached to them," she said.

Agnes came many times that month. She taught me to laugh in bed, and that there's no difference between giving and taking. Happy birthday.

My uncle offered me a job in his store. In the back of the Photo Lab there were five racks of expensive stolen coats. I asked Feldstein why they were there and he told me a friend left them because he didn't have room.

But I knew a lot about commerce by then. Feldstein had had me running numbers, or being his bagman. I was a big kid, and I'd worked the docks before Archie Winstin had his first paper route. (Incidentally, he made a lot of money off that route, because I showed him how to run it. There are always a lot of things you can do on the side, other people to involve; no one trusts anyone else, which is how you could turn a buck. There are two kinds of work, and mostly I did the legal kind.)

I was the only kid I knew that wasn't a dangerous little hood at heart.

About the coats. I called Frankie, a sort of wholesaler I knew, to look at them. He came after closing and offered me three grand.

"I'm not going to cut Feldstein's throat for that kind of dough," I said.

"Am I a charity organization? No, I'm a businessman."

"Then do business elsewhere, you cheap small-time crook." I had to act tough with Frankie, because he was always holding out. Especially because he thought he could walk all over me because I was just a kid.

"Okay," he said. "Since they're from out of town, I can work the insurance scam with you."

"Fine. Fifty percent for me. And not a word to Feldstein about it."

There was a noise at the back door; it was either rats or my uncle Feldstein.

He was with two hairy, stupid-looking guys. One of them was probably going bald, also less stupid, and obviously the boss.

When Feldstein walked in, he saw me posing with a fur. "You look like a princess, now put it back."

The other guys looked annoyed, but not enough to say something. The bossy guy was snooping around the coats like the snub-nosed shark he was. The stupider guy looked like he was carrying a B-52 bomber under his jacket.

"This your friend?" I asked my uncle.

"Yeah, this is my friend."

"He's got more room now?"

"That's right. He might take them back now."

The friend turned and showed his shark teeth.

"How come his friend's carrying a gun?" I asked.

Stupider patted his left tit. Feldstein laughed.

Frankie was in a corner being invisible.

Feldstein and his friend whispered bad things to each other, sounding like two snakes fucking. Then the friend looked at Stupider, who pulled his piece. Feldstein lost his head and rushed him with his hands up like a linebacker. A shot was fired. Stupider spun around with the gun still cold in his hand, looked at Frankie in the corner, and faded out.

"Beat it," Frankie said solemnly to my uncle's pale balding friend, and he did.

Feldstein sat on the floor, useless with surprise.

Stupider was dead.

Shooting someone has to do with the business, and when I was doing a job, I didn't let it bother me if I had to do it. Later, months later sometimes, I'd remember with a vivid slow-motion clarity. I never blamed myself, but I still felt very sad. I'd punish myself by thinking of the widow an' kids, the ailing grandmudda, but I never did anything corny like send a check. I didn't even know half the guys. Some I knew.

So what does a kid like me do for the next seven years? Drop out of school, work for Feldstein, take the equivalency, quit Feldstein and go to medical college in Mexico, drop out after two years and work for Feldstein, quit again and go to the Art

Students League. Feldstein, Feldstein, Feldstein, and then the scholarship. Maybe there was something in the nature of revenge for Feldstein, getting me in his line of business and not letting go.

On my twenty-first birthday, Feldstein stuck his head in the door frame of the studio. "Psst." Feldstein would never set foot in a place like that, out of respect.

He took me to the Hickory House coffee shop on Fifty-seventh Street. "I could take you someplace fancy. But you can put it in your memoirs that your uncle Feldstein took you to the lousy Hickory House."

Feldstein was always generous. He'd trusted me with everything since the deal with Frankie and the coats. He needed me, and I needed him like a hole in the head and I knew it. I'd been running from Feldstein for a long time.

"Need some dough?" he asked.

"Everything's fine," I said.

"I mean, I could give you a little job. Wouldn't take too much time."

His little jobs were never easy, but I was still living off the last one. I'd been wondering what I'd do when that ran out; I'd quit Feldstein more than a year before, for the last time, I'd said.

"I can count on you's why. It's all planned, but I still need you. It's complicated."

Habits are hard to break. He was my uncle.

"But never again."

Feldstein smiled. He'd heard that before.

It was 5 a.m. in the morning at night. Mr. Alvarado was the biggest complication so far, and he was sitting next to me in a truck stop near Palomar. He was nervous.

We had crossed the border in Southern California because it should have been easier than crossing in Texas. Alvarado wasn't Mexican, but being small and dark, he got the border guards excited anyway.

We were hauling a van full of household goods, stolen paintings, and cocaine worth ten million dollars. There were some horrible reproductions thrown in along with Mr. Laurel's genuine Goyas and Rembrandts. Alvarado's cocaine was stuffed into the frames of the fakes. All of this had been my uncle's idea.

Except for Alvarado. It was a neat idea to swing two deals at one time, but Alvarado decided he had to come along. He was a young guy. His family had a good reputation in my uncle's circle. This was his first big deal, and he was more afraid of getting ripped off by Feldstein or his buyer than he was scared of Customs and Immigration. But he was a scared kind of a guy. I wondered why his family was making him do this. Maybe it was some kind of ritual, and if you come out alive, they let you fuck some virgin. Maybe Alvarado was the virgin. I decided he was. It's just another way of categorizing people.

So a guard hassled us at the border. Nothing but routine early-morning suspicion. I told Alvarado, "He's looking for the sixteen brothers and sisters he thinks are *between* the paintings." But Alvarado was nervous and got out of the van.

The next step was meeting Mr. Laurel near Palomar and then taking both these guys to meet Feldstein and the buyers at a farm outside San Pedro. It seemed too complicated, and, I thought, I should be the one who is running this thing.

Alvarado came over and started to whisper, which is one thing not to do. It gets these guys mad. The guard checking the stuff in the back came over.

"What's all that stuffer?"

"Furniture for my new house," I said.

"Where d'ya buyum?"

"Zacapa," I said.

"Have receipts?"

I showed him, and he ordered us out of the car. He called for some help, and a bunch of boys began to dismantle the dashboard. I didn't mind so long as we weren't going to be late, but Alvarado was jumpy and the guards kept taking steady looks at him.

"Stop advertising yourself," I said.

"Maybe I should have worn a tie," he said.

"Maybe I should have worn tails and a ten-gallon hat," I said. Alvarado nodded seriously, not getting it.

While we were waiting for Laurel at the truck stop near Palomar, I ordered an egg-salad sandwich. I still had sand caught in my teeth from the drive across the desert, but food was food. I didn't care about the stuff, but you tend to let down your guard if you don't eat.

Alvarado ordered a coffee.

"You should eat," I said.

"I can't. When you can't, you can't."

There was just no telling how long we were going to have to wait for Laurel, who was already an hour late, or Feldstein, either.

"Sometimes you better eat anyhow," I said.

"When you can't, you can't," he said. We were both talking bullshit simple Latino wisdom. Short phrases that are supposed to stand for big ideas. Doesn't work that way. Half-baked.

He looked at me like I was some kind of specimen of desert-animal life. The kind that's well suited for the conditions. "I envy you," he said. "You're a natural for this business."

A tall fat man in a rough white suit creased the doorway of the truck stop. Here was trouble. I had a bad feeling for Alvarado.

"Good morning," Laurel greeted us, and I knew he'd been up for hours. Which didn't explain his being late.

We all had a copy of Feldstein's map. Giving everyone a map was unnecessary, I thought. He should have let me plan this from the start. From now on, I thought, that's the way it's going to be. Then: What the hell am I thinking about? This is the last time.

Laurel made sure it was a long ride. Leaning across Alvarado's body to chat, he forced Alvarado to push against my right arm. Steering was difficult.

"Business is great, eh, Alvarez?" he said. Cheerful like the Chamber of fucking Commerce. (You can meet a lot of tough characters hanging around there. Con men and CIA types.)

"Michael here's a painter," Laurel said. "That's a fine business to be in, eh, Alvarez?"

"Alvarado," Alvarado said.

"Ha ha. Seriously, he should stick to that. Painting's not dangerous."

"So who's afraid?" I blustered. Laurel had a strange effect. Whenever you tried to show him how tough you were, you came off looking like Winnie the Pooh in a huff. Laurel was wearing white, but he was a real tough guy, and he didn't have to let you know to let you know.

When a jeep crossed the road a few yards ahead and stopped in the middle, I knew what Laurel had been doing all morning.

I wondered if Alvarado's mother was going to get some kind of a pension. My job wasn't to protect anyone except Feldstein and the merchandise.

Alvarado asked pitifully, "What's this?"

"Probably my uncle checking up," I said.

Laurel and I got out to give his hoods a clear shot. The hoods didn't miss.

I turned to Laurel and said, "If you're planning a surprise party for me, you'll find I'm not easy to kill." Bluster, bluster.

"I have no doubt," Laurel said. Trustless confidence. I thought, He's killed his father and fucked his mother. He's fucked his sister. He's gotten it from every whore he wanted, and for nothing.

Laurel's hoods wrapped up the body before it bled too much, and we left.

Feldstein was late. We found an old campfire and started it up while we waited.

"Tell me," Laurel said, crouching but not sitting so he wouldn't dirty the seat of his pants, "why do you play these dangerous games?"

"Dangerous for who?"

He smiled. I told you the effect that kind of talk has on Laurel. "Is it money? I'm just curious. Money's a good reason. I like money. That's why I'm here. I don't trust anyone with my money."

Laurel liked listening to himself talk, and so did I. But guys who fuck their mothers are totally selfish. Guys like that take exactly what they want. Guys like that start early and they never stop protecting it.

"You have to make a choice sooner or later," he said. "One life or the other."

"What do you know about my choices?" It just seemed like one of those conversations people have while they're waiting for Feldstein and the buyers.

"You're an artist and you're playing at gangster."

"What makes you think I'm playing," I said, trying to narrow my eyes.

Laurel laughed. "I don't mean you're an amateur. I'm not saying that. But if this was your real life, I'd know everything there is to know about you. And if you do become a pro, I'll know where you sleep and who you fuck and what your little finger is thinking even before you do."

"I free-lance," I said.

"For your uncle?"

29

"Right."

"Blood is thicker than water?"

"Right."

This guy, I thought, isn't all that concerned with my future. He certainly isn't dumb. Or maybe he's lucky in his choices of conversation. But he's trying to tease my mind away from . . . he's going to blow someone away. Not Feldstein. One of the buyers. Maybe he's got someone on the farm. Watch his hands, watch for a signal.

"You should stick to painting."

"Yeah?"

"Otherwise you'll get killed."

"Who'll kill me? You?"

He shrugged. "Not me."

I looked over his shoulder into the woods behind the farm.

There's an eighty-two-year-old model at the Art Students League and she's been there for sixty-one years. She's very famous because she's posed for a lot of great painters. Last month she modeled for me, and I thought she was beautiful. She models for a lot of people. What I thought while I was sitting by the fire on Feldstein's farm is that she represents continuity. Continuity seemed important. And with all these bodies, what kind of continuity could Feldstein offer?

Two cars pulled up and Feldstein got out of one of them. He had the coke buyer with him. The art buyer was alone in another car; he was a Spanish-looking guy, thin and young.

"Where's Mr. Alvarez?" Feldstein asked. He was always bad with names.

"Laurel's here instead," I said.

"But he was so anxious to be here himself, that's so . . ."

Feldstein was momentarily baffled, but not so the others. The coke dealer was petulant: So you killed him, right? The art dealer walked away.

Laurel and the coke dealer met privately, at an unfriendly impasse. Laurel was trying to raise the price.

Feldstein was trying to catch my attention, but I wasn't looking. If you look at him with his gesticulating eyebrows and glances brimming over with meaning, you're lost. I was on duty, and I also was thinking about something else— continuity.

The coke dealer wouldn't budge. "A deal's a deal."

"But your bargain wasn't with me," said Laurel.

"I didn't come all the way down here for this bullshit and I'm not going back empty."

He pulled a gun from his pocket. He had the right idea about Laurel, but he didn't have enough information. Laurel raised both hands over his head and closed one to a fist. Now I had seen the signal. A high-caliber pistol shot rang from the middle range. The coke dealer was so dead he'd never even existed.

The art dealer was more than happy to take everything off Laurel's hands. Laurel's hood dragged away the body, leaving matted weeds and a pool of blood. The bullet fired at that distance had wobbled and left a large pudding instead of a hole in a chest.

Laurel handed Feldstein five grand.

"What do you call this?"

"Your commission," Laurel said. He walked away, toward wherever men in white linen suits disappear to.

"You fucking cheap cheat," Feldstein shouted. "Stop him, will ya!" Feldstein shouted, but knowing what I did, the person I had to stop was Feldstein.

He rushed at Laurel, arms high. I should have tackled him, but I didn't. I was thinking about continuity and the eighty-two-year-old model.

Feldstein got one bullet in the lower abdominal cavity. He didn't die right off, and I cradled his head in my lap.

"You're not mad?" he asked.

"No."

"I should have let you plan it from the start."

31

Laurel's hood waited for the new body.

"There's a model at the school," I said. "She's been there sixty-one years."

Feldstein was dead.

I got in his car.

I was finally rid of Feldstein.

It was too bad I had to lose him this way.

the backswing
of the
slugger

Baseball has always been everything, but baseball isn't the question anymore. I've become a fractional human being all by my own doing, and now, goddamn it, that fraction's been snuffed out, too.

At the end of August the manager of the St. Louis farm team in Orthrup, New York, called me into his office. I wasn't too surprised to be going to the majors—it had taken longer than I'd expected. I figured I'd have to say good-bye to my new girlfriend, if I could get hold of her. I didn't care either way. The manager, Tim Bixy—a name like that, can you believe it?—said I wasn't good enough to play pro ball and I should go home. It was like being told I was dead by the funeral director while no one else was watching. There wasn't even someone to look at for consolation.

I have a lot of trouble liking myself, and I don't doubt that you will, too. I'm a mean and cynical person, and that's rough when you're young. It makes you look shallow. People say all kinds of sincere bullshit, like "I'm trying to find myself." I envy them a little, because they're honest to themselves. But

33

I say, "Yeah, well, why don't you look under your hat for starters."

I'd never let anyone else do what I've done to myself.

Last Friday, I tried fucking my new girlfriend up her asshole. I was past the point of asking. I just pulled my prick out of her cunt and tried. I tried for damn near an hour. She was in tears. Grinding my teeth and practically making my hair fall out, sweat pouring into my eyes. A last angry rush. I gave up and we lay side by side. We rested. She begged me not to try again.

My new girlfriend is very new. It's August and I've been in Orthrup since late June. I'm honestly surprised it's lasted this long, but maybe that's because she didn't know me very well. Or because she doesn't have much else to look forward to in Orthrup. My old girlfriend was different.

My family got rich from baseball because my father is a good listener. He didn't pay any attention until he came to see me play once. I played first base that year, because I was the tallest kid. Tall and thin, not much of a wing. That developed later. My mother (she came to watch every week) said to him, "Look at the mess he's made around first base with his spikes. He's so excited."

Between every pitch, I did a little trip around the base, the path, the edge of the grass, picked up pebbles, ripped uneven clumps out by their roots, smoothed the packed dirt with my spikes, rocked back and forth, heel-toe, heel-toe, until the pitcher started up again. If ever I loved someone, it was baseball. I loved the *things* about it. The moments when nothing seemed to be happening. The feeling of the fine dust settling in my nostrils was as important to me as the base runners. That's what I miss the most, the baseballness of baseball, and I realize that as the years went on, I let it slip away and didn't notice.

I hit a home run that game, like almost every game. I had a strong swing. I drove with my hips, shoulders, lips, my unmoving eyes, determinedly into the ball, the sweet spot on the bat. I've always had pop in my bat.

You can't see the ball at all the last seven feet to the plate. Legions of Little League managers say, "Watch the ball hit your bat," but you can't possibly do it. You can distract yourself trying. I've never seen a home run jump off my bat, but I've felt them in my hands, on the sweet spot on the bat.

My father heard me hit. And since we lost that day, he also heard the furious silence on my face. He must have thought, Why does this game make so much noise? His feet, his hands, his face.

Imagine a famous political columnist in the dugout of the New York Yankees on a colorless spring day, asking questions like a jerk. My father. This man who once asked the President, "Why do you love children?" and who produced that famous answer, three columns long. Who once asked another question, "What would you say to Karl Marx if you met him today?" In short, a stupid man who asked stupid questions. But I give him credit, because baseball is a game of stupid questions. Question: "Why does Stottlemyre wear a long-sleeved sweatshirt even in this heat?" Answer: "To keep his arm warm." And they say good managers are geniuses. Earl Weaver, a famous genius, said, "I play him every day because he's good."

I hate my old girlfriend. I have always hated my old girlfriends. You know what I said to my new girlfriend? I told her my old girlfriend never wanted to suck my cock. I said she

35

always asked me to eat her out, but she never liked to suck my cock.

I hate my sister because she never fucked me.

My father took us to Fort Lauderdale every spring from '71 to '75. I had a catch with Willie Mays one morning. Just until his arm came around. I played catch with ballplayers' kids, other sportswriters' kids, just kids like me. My father was a sportswriter then, even though he despised the title. He still wanted to be called a journalist. My mother and sister sometimes met us for lunch. Who knows or cares what else they did.

I had a great time as a kid. I was a fucking fool. The old men who watched the game said I had enthusiasm, and they were right. I got up in the morning and I played baseball and watched baseball, and sometimes I had lunch with my parents, usually when my mother had had a shit fit the night before and said baseball was breaking up the family. My stupid sister sat there during those tirades, seriously nodding. But I figured she didn't care any more than I did. She was just taking sides. For a while I took the trouble to wonder why my sister was never on my side anymore, but then I gave up. After lunch, I played baseball.

In the old neighborhood, before my father used to take us to Fort Lauderdale every spring, I played baseball on our Little League team, called the Kings because the King Apartment Buildings were our sponsor. It was lucky, because there were kids that played for a funeral home and a kosher butcher, and I say, Who could take himself seriously with a name like one of those on your uniform?

I used to get the bus out to the field early. I mean, early like before the first worm could even be coaxed out of bed by the very earliest bird. I would get the bus that was still standing in the terminal from the night before and wait for the driver and the dispatcher to come in from the coffee shop. I'd sit way in the back and put my glove on the seat next to me so that no one would sit there. There wasn't much chance of that, because I was usually the only passenger for the first half of the run. As we got closer to the shopping center in Jackson Heights, the bus started to fill up with old ladies, and then after we passed it, the bus got nearly empty again.

One time, an oval-headed old man in a loose, dark suit climbed on at the terminal. I had him pegged right off as a scout for the Giants or Braves. When he got off two stops before the end, I was disappointed, but I hardly missed my stride. I figured he needed a cup of coffee. Fuck him. Fuck scouts.

The field was wedged up against the bay between La Guardia and Butler Aviation Field, on a rocky bunch of acres owned by the city. Out on the bay was Rikers Island, a prison. I always dreamed of hitting a ball out there, an impossibility, and beaning a con with it. Alone, of course, I chucked rocks up in the air and caught them in my trusty glove. I practiced my swing with a short stick I found by the water. It was an hour before Vinnie ever showed up, and then some other guys with a real ball. I had forgotten all about the scout back then. That's the kind of thing I've lost track of. Those days, all I think about is the scouts.

Shit.

I'd been lying in bed with my new girlfriend all weekend, though at her insistence as far apart in a twin bed as physically possible. Friday, I'd tried to fuck her up the ass again and we hadn't been outside since. We had pizza and soda delivered four times, and I made her answer the door. I wasn't getting out of bed for anything, and my girlfriend looks like a real slut. Especially in her bare feet, in one of my T-shirts that's too big for her. Let the asshole get a look at what I can still have, I was thinking, of course.

*   *   *

Rusty Staub had just been traded to the Tigers, and my father was sitting with him in the dugout. I don't know how I could stand it, because my father was so stupid. For some kids, it's a treat to watch their fathers at work, but not for me. He asked questions with his hands folded like a napkin on his notepad and stared at Staub. I could see Staub laughing inside.

My old girlfriend had nothing to do with baseball. She was there, but she didn't have anything to do with it. She was there, though, a blurry bridge between two parts of my life.

"It's too hot outside," I said to my new girlfriend. I wanted to tell her more about my old girlfriend. I wanted to stifle my old girlfriend to death with the thick yarn of my voice.

My old girlfriend left me my junior year. She was a cheerleader, and she left me for a quarterback.

Can you beat it?

I hate her so much I can't remember ever having liked her.

It might be easy to blame my father. He stepped in and spoiled the game for me. He took the fun out. But it's always too easy to blame fathers. Besides, he's too stupid to have had an impact.

My arm was as strong as ever, and I was playing shortstop. I was deep in the hole, grinding my teeth and hoping the guy was going to hit it to me so I could gun him down and end the game.

Frank was pitching, and he deserved to get the win. He wasn't the greatest pitcher I ever saw, and he didn't even have his usual stuff that day, but we needed him to come through and he was pulling it off. He was fighting like hell.

We gave him a big cushion early, mostly because of a three-run homer I hit in the first. After three, we were up 7–2, and it looked like a laugher. But their third pitcher was setting us down, and their shortstop was having a great game. His name was Chuckie Burek, and his father, Chuckie, Sr., was the manager. Chuckie Burek was an asshole who'd as easily punch your teeth out with the ball as tag you on the hip. I hated him, the other top shortstop in the league.

Every inning, Frank got into trouble and then got out of it, but not without giving up a run. But anyway, it was the last inning and we were only up by two, and they had two runners in scoring position.

Vinnie and I visited Frank on the mound. The catcher's always got to know what's going on. It's in their nature. I was there because I felt it was important for me to put in an appearance. The three of us stood there. It was three guys on a little hill, no wind, nothing to say. Everyone is allowed their little drama. There were no words exchanged finally. I patted Frank on the rump with my glove, winked at Vinnie, the only other kid from the neighborhood gang to make the team, and then we went back to our positions.

Frank was alone on the mound again, the ball tucked away from the batter. He was concentrating on the target and breathing heavily. He had a huge round chest to draw power from, and a long pitcher's face.

The ball should have been past me. But I was too fast, too good that day. Almost on the outfield grass, I planted my foot and threw to first.

The ball sang; one moment it hovered in place, the next it was in Thatcher's glove at first.

Like in a cartoon.

The game was over on an outstanding play by me. I had won the game with my bat and my hands and my arm.

My new girlfriend asked me what happened. Since I'd

known her, she hadn't asked me any questions, and even better, she didn't expect me to talk.

A week before the major-league draft, I took a walk with my sister, who was my only friend. I loved her to the roots of my hair, and I couldn't forgive her for hating me. I tried to hold her hand, but she jerked it away. She stared straight ahead.

"You're such a dick," she said. "I can't believe it, but you're worse than Dad. I used to have hope for you. You used to be a human being even though you were a shitty brother. All you care about is baseball, baseball, baseball. And yourself. You tore yourself apart from everything, from your family, from Tom, from Crane."

Who the hell was Crane?

I was claimed by the Cardinals in the twenty-first round of the June Amateur Draft. It was the wrong round, the wrong league, and a standard contract. But I signed it anyhow.

"A very small percentage of kids get picked at all. You should be proud," my father said.

He was right. But even he knew it wasn't good enough.

I took a dinky apartment in Orthrup, which is where the Cardinal farm team plays in the New York Penn League. It's the lowest of the low, but I figured they'd recognize their mistake and call me up to St. Louis soon. I figured I'd demand a trade at the end of the season.

I chased my new girlfriend around with a baseball bat. I yelled and slipped on a pizza box and made so much noise in general that someone called her brother and he came around with three friends. She told him everything was all right, go away. I sat in one corner of the room, holding the bat, and she sat in the opposite corner, watching me and catching her breath. She didn't have the brains or something to get a knife. She didn't even know it, but for a minute I would have let her do it to me.

So where does a guy go when he's lost everything?

I don't mean this to sound like despair, but I better get some answers soon.

tHe meMOiRS OF YOuNge michaEL MissInge

A little while after they started America, Lafitte started his own country in Texas. They let him. Lafitte had had a lot to do with America, people owed him. He called the land Campeche in honor of a great pirate captain.

"Campeche, he was advanced for his time."

"Because he was an atheist?" I asked.

"Because he treated the men like equals, he shared evenly with them. My good little friend, he was the devil." Jean laughed and squeezed my thigh, bare below my blue-jean cutoffs.

I was an assistant to banditry on the high seas, the pillaging of towns, debauchery, graft, and heroism. I loved the devil under a full moon. A stiff cock, a strong breeze, the spray of a Spaniard's blood upon my face. Like Morgan to Mansfield and later Exemelin to Morgan, I was Missinge to Lafitte. His below-deck secretary, ship's surgeon, and lover.

I told Jean I didn't like shitting off the prow, because I was afraid of falling overboard into my own shit—he said my upbringing was fucked up, but his was no better, to judge by his behavior. He used more toilet paper than anyone on board, and never used his hand.*

The first time Jean cast eyes on the coastline of Louisiana, I was next to him. It had just been sold to Jefferson, and Lafitte thought it was a great deal (though the anti-Federalists among the crew felt the President had no constitutional mandate for that sort of action).

Jean was about to step forward onto a log and hop onto the shore—the log was in fact a treacherous Seminole Indian[†] lying facedown as a trap. I drew my gun quickly and shot him.

I earned Jean's trust then, as well as his love.

Jean often spanked me, and I cried. He reminded me of my late uncle Edward Teach. Both had black beards, though Jean was by far the handsomer.

I cried when Jean took a mistress, and I howled with anger when she got with child.

"Fuck this shit," I sniffed, packing my surgeon's tools.

Lafitte sat on the edge of the bed, hands on bony knees.

"React, you anal bastard!" I wanted to be talked out of it.

"You know," he said softly, occasionally raising his eyes to mine, pausing deliberately, "I will be so hurt if you leave. But you—you are younge. It would be harder for you if I had just died. If you could never see me again. Now we will both live, and soon you will remember me fondly and the pain will diminish. In a year or two."

That French smoothie. I was indeed younge, and could no more face two years of pain than the heart-wrenching thought of his death.

"Don't manipulate me," I said, but already my anger was passing.

"I love you," he said. "No woman can come between us."

No woman could come between us, no woman captured in

---

* "Show them you're a man/wipe it with your han'."—Old pirate jingle.
† This Seminole imitation of crocodile behavior is at the root of the word *somnolent*.

a wealthy town, no woman married or kept; no, I was safe from these. But we were to be challenged by another type of woman, a daughter he had fathered.

At table on board, I always sat next to Jean, our knees touching. But he shied away from public displays of affection; as I say, his upbringing was no less anal than mine.

"The French Revolution was for freedom. America's?! That was a taxpayers' revolt," said le Basque derisively.

"On the contrary," Lafitte countered. He was a big fan of America, and Andy Jackson in particular. "There are larger ideals expressed there—enterprise and opportunity. The pursuit of happiness."

To that, the big pilot spat meanly on the floor. I put my hand on Jean's leg—but Lafitte was Lafitte, and he was the most successful pirate of the post-1700 era for good reason: he had command over his emotions.

Talk of violence and the rape of young women is largely sensationalistic fabrication.

This is by no means an apologia. Piracy can stand on its own merits. In the beginning, we were a random force, a free-market hazard, that affected the imperialist countries but little. We were less of a problem, say, than yellow fever in Panama.

But Mansfield's nephew sank a small Spanish armada in 1715, and suddenly we were getting offers from the British and the French (never from the Spanish. Anyhow, they were too good a target. Their clumsy bureaucracy, beginning with the Casa de Contratación, which they passed in 1503, was the symbol of frustrated seriousness, their futile and stubborn attempt at national greatness. The result of fixing maximum ship weights, minimum artillery requirements, and other safety features was the regular bribing of inspectors, the renting of cannons for the purpose of passing inspection, and the irresponsible piling up of slaves, precious stones, colonial goods stacked in the life rafts and locked in the hulls of the sagging and sluggish ships).

We eventually paid duties and honorariums to the governors of islands (Tortuga, Hispaniola, Barataria) and, in some cases, protection money; so the War of 1812 was not the first skirmish in which we proved a decisive power.

Jean was out of jail then and had been recruited to fight for General Andrew Jackson, to whom he taught his triangle formation.

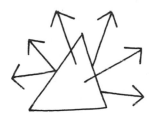

Jackson had objected, "Clausewitz writes—"

"Damn that Kraut!" Lafitte interrupted. "When was the last time the Germans won a war?"

His flanks protected, the British systematic as bricks, Andy destroyed the flower of the king's army. Jackson later told Jean that beating them so soundly destroyed any British ideas of ever gaining another foothold in North America.

The war was supposed to be over. But Jackson (being a military man) suspected a ruse, arrested the Louisiana state legislature, entire, charged them with abetting the enemy, and slapped them around in the cell.

When the armistice was officially announced, he was obligated to let them out, and they did the logical thing, arrested him back and slapped *him* around in the cell.

"What a banana republic," I said.

"Give them a chance," Jean growled.

He was a great American patriot.

Jackson was tried by a jury of his peers and fined a con-
siderable sum. He made a silly speech on the courthouse
steps (a traditional speechmaking arena, respected in the Con-
stitution). He asked pirates to follow his example, respect the
law, and stop operating out of New Orleans.

We took up a collection, and Jackson got his thousand
simoleons back. We stopped raiding American shipping, and
Jean started his own country. Jackson slaughtered the Semi-
noles as a personal favor—and a good public-relations ploy—
and became the seventh president of the United States.

Lafitte was a great captain and strategist. He had won more
booty and raided more towns, boarded more Spanish galle-
ons, than any other pirate. You can look it up. He commanded
a fleet of thirty-five ships, enough men and supplies for large-
scale operations, enough room and force to carry off huge
treasures. He had connections with wholesalers on an international scale. Lafitte's reputation is legendary.

So you demand cruelty and violence.

Lafitte's fleet sailed one month along the Yucatán Canal,
as it was called, and through the Golfe du Honduras. We
stopped on Sainte Cataline—then under French dominion—
to hunt livestock. During the break, Lafitte revealed his plan
to the assembled pirates: the sack of Panama City! It meant
crossing the straits on foot and by canoe, then crossing the
plain and attacking the fort, capturing the Spanish gold in
transit from Peru and Chile, carrying it back across the way
we came, hoping that meanwhile our ships were safe in the
Golfe d'Urabá.

Jean had confided to me that it was to be his last big
campaign.

Lafitte was a showman: he asked the assembly to deliber-
ate without him, and he left the stage.

Bartholemew Rogers, a captain of one of the warships, came along to his tent a few minutes later.

"O syphilitic bastard," he began, "how many men will we lose to the fever? To the beasts and priests, and pests and animals? The Indians? How many at the fort itself? Who will be left to carry back the gold?"

"*Porc!*" said Lafitte. "You suffer from SIDA* of the brain."

"I speak from my heart," said the trembling Rogers.

"Just so," Jean cried out, and before my eyes pulled his dagger from his belt and swiftly cut into Rogers's chest. He carved through the ribs without even scratching his blade, loosened the heart from its moorings, seized it with his hand, and stuffed it into the astonished man's open mouth.

Cruelty and violence.

"Rogers wasn't wrong," Jean said to me. "But I have a surprise no one can know about."

I didn't wait for him to elaborate; the bloody talk had turned me on.

"Take me like a woman," I said. I prostrated myself, and he tore off my shorts.

During our love play, the greed-swollen pirates voted overwhelmingly in favor of Jean's plan.

Panama City had gotten wind of our approach, and the governor of the city came to meet us at the head of twenty-five hundred men.

We prayed silently and uttered, in one voice, Amen. Jean deployed the men in the triangle formation.

Governor Juan Pérez de Guzmán's secret weapon was the buffalo that grazed wildly on the prairie—which his gauchos

---

* The French acronym for Acquired Immune Deficiency Syndrome, now known as Tim Spiker's Disease, after the inventor of the vaccine.

had managed to corral. The governor seriously doubted that a band of brigands could outfight his highly trained soldiers; and yet . . .

It was lucky for him he had extended himself that option, for as the drama of the battle unrolled like a spool of film, he needed that last resort. He gave the signal, and the gauchos began to fire furiously into the air, chasing and hooting the buffalo to a trot, to a gallop, and finally to a stampede in our direction.

Our quaintly colorful shirts were like tiny red flags for the mass running and stumbling across the plain. We stopped firing and dumbly watched them grow nearer, thinking vaguely about whites of eyes, the leader of the pack, and other useful scoutlike admonitions.

Lafitte, the great commander, pointed his pistol to the sky, fired, and shouted for us to do the same. We did; the confused beasts slowly came to a halt, then dispersed, grazing between the two armies and mooing loquaciously.*

We then spent three weeks loading gold onto mules, raping innocent women and children, and holding prominent citizens for ransom—who came from as far away as Maracaibo and Curaçao.

"Next trip, Venezuela," Lafitte said to the men, who cheered and raped some more.

I worried about the time we were wasting; Spain's Atlantic armada was arriving to cut off our escape. Jean laughed and leaned forward suddenly in his chair. He took my thigh in his rough hands and squeezed until I thought an artery would burst.

"You're hurting me," I said.

---

* Hence the lyric in the "Marseillaise": Hear the mooing of the ferocious soldiers (*Entendez-vous . . . mugir ces féroces soldats*).

He released me and got up and left. Alone, I rubbed my wounded leg resentfully and rued this way of life.

When we arrived at the mouth of the last canal leading out to the Atlantic, we could see from our gold-laden canoes the masts of the Spanish armada. We had remained unnoticed.

When night fell, we drifted closer to the coast, waiting for the stars to set and dawn's thick fog. Quietly as we could, we stole aboard our own boats.

The Spanish awoke to heavy artillery fire from our cannons, and as the sun burned off the fog, we saw two Spanish ships sliding under the water.

Still, there seemed no reason for the Spanish not to advance and destroy our little flotilla. But rather than maneuvering toward us, the Spanish admiral formed a circle, as if surrounded.

And indeed he was, for behind him had crept seven heavy ships flying American colors; Jean hoisted an old American flag he had on board (already two stars behind).

It was a great reunion, at first. Short and balding, a falcon-faced landlubber, our beloved Andrew Jackson, came aboard. Jean ordered a feast; we always ate sumptuously, but particularly after a successful raid.

"How much this time?"

"Well, Andrew, maybe six hundred thousand pieces of eight. One raft went to the crocodiles"—there was laughter all round the table—"a dozen head of cattle and other provisions, some interesting works of philosophy, the idealists, and some Cervantes—"

Jackson poked at his food and then interrupted, "I'm not interested in all that. How much in all?"

Jean smiled gently and Jackson looked sullenly at his plate.

"You know, nobody paid us for our work during the British war."

"Madison was a fool," Jackson admitted.

"I work for myself these days."

"Jean. Monsieur Lafitte. We have an arrangement."

"Yes. I harass the Spanish. That is my end of the bargain. You protect me. That is your end. *Punto final.* I am glad that while earning a living, I can serve America's interests."

Jackson coughed.

Lafitte said, "President General Wéshington had the correct idea, staying out of foreign entanglements."

"America is just an upstart country," I said. "They don't do business like the English or the French." I was repeating what I'd often heard above deck, particularly from the older men, companions in '14, when Lafitte got gypped by Madison.

Jean glared at me.

"On the contrary," Jackson said.

He hated Washington, but bore him respect.

"Washington and company were excellent businessmen. They needed out from under Britain's great bureaucracy, the constraints, tariffs, red tape."

Jackson was a general, born hater of the red-tape factory, an anti-Federalist if there ever was one, but also a military man, that is, a believer in leadership, the *status quo ante*, central control, and, above all, discipline.

"The Revolution," he muttered, adding, almost in a whisper, "Can you imagine fat George, a sack of potatoes atop a white horse, trying to be Napoleon—"

His giggling got the better of him, he couldn't go on, and Jean squirmed in his seat, forking his pheasant and hating Jackson.

"President Tax-Break," Jackson burst out laughing.

I snickered. It was more than Lafitte could handle, and he jumped off his seat. He was getting old, nearing forty.

"America is the best damn country in the world," he spluttered, "and George Wéshington was its first president, and he never told a lie."

"I never said he did," Jackson said sensibly.

*   *   *

Andy slept on board that night with us, and I fell asleep wondering whether or not to go in his stateroom, which is how I missed out on fucking the future president.

In the morning, we lifted anchor for Louisiana. We had the customary breakfast together with Jean's kid brother Pierre, but Jean and Jackson were oddly formal; after the meal, they said good-bye and Jackson boarded a skiff that brought him across to his own ship. For three weeks, our ships sailed together without another shuttle being made, without even one wave from our deck to his.

Lafitte spoke a lot about his daughter, Denise-Jeannette, talked about sending her to school in Europe, worried about the lack of appropriate companionship at Campeche.

"Piracy is a dead issue," he said. "We shall move to the Continent. Pierre will come with us, and we shall conduct the honest trade of stolen goods: cocoa, rum, pineapple, potatoes. We'll use Pierre's contacts in Brussels."

"What about your money?" I said.

Following Lafitte's instructions, I had disposed of more than fifty thousand U.S. dollars in various banks and establishments in New York and Pennsylvania. There were also several hundred pieces of gold invested around New Orleans.

"You may have to return once in a while," he said. I sensed that this was a ruse to get rid of me occasionally, when he wanted to be alone with Denise-Jeannette. Naturally, I was jealous, but I was trying to deal with it.

Upon our return to Campeche, Jean made a speech to the men, a maudlin, cliché-laden talk about how the world had changed and we with it, etc., a rambling, almost senile exhibition of declining intellect. There are certain private associations from which one cannot (easily) resign. But as Lafitte's speech grew in theoretical intricacies of disconnected trivia, I heard whispers—syphilis, arteriosclerosis, ossification. Jean smiled from the podium, childlike and seemingly childish.

If this cunning was his most evolved intellectual maneuver within an extraordinary and emotive society, it was also a moment when theatrics fused with the being of the actor, forever changing him and the people in his intimate circle.

Neither Denise-Jeannette nor I could ever recapture the awe with which we had regarded him before. We began to love him, jealously, as a precious old man, a font of ancient secrets. A codger.

[I I]

Pierre was assigned to New York, after all, as head of a Jackson for President committee.

"Here are some letters of introduction for Brussels," Pierre said coldly.

Jean had always supplied the goods, taken all the chances. Pierre had traveled to Europe.

"Pierre did time with me in New Orleans," Jean defended.

Denise-Jeannette was a beautiful fifteen-year-old girl, perpetually surprised by the beauty which perpetually surrounded her, or which she perpetually emanated, or which was perpetually created around her to please her.

The crossing to Belgium was intolerable.

She demanded time from Jean, and she often got it at my expense. I spent most afternoons in a lounge chair aft, keeping up with the reading Jean insisted his secretary had to do. Meanwhile, he explained to her the naval charts, corridors, and currents, while both stared dreamily off the bow. Likewise, many nights.

One afternoon, as they passed me, I looked up from my book and said, "This union too is fragile and corruptible."

"Hume," Jean approved.

"Missinge," I said.

Denise-Jeannette looked at me curiously.

In Brussels, I decided to leave him. When Jean walked into my room, I was afraid to talk to him. I had wanted to leave him before and had let him talk me out of it.

He tried to embrace me, and I avoided his arm. He implored me to take a walk with him. I realized suddenly that there was nothing he could do to change me.

He took my hand and I let him hold it. Outside, bearded men holding large flat portfolios, horse-powered carriages, and philosophers crowded the streets with the density of human activity.

We entered a café to discuss the future terms of my employment.

"I want my own apartment," I added. None of my demands were excessive; I had come cheap, and he had lots of dough.

"I may change my name," he said.

Jean ordered two large coffees *mit Schlag.*

A bearded philosopher was getting his shoulders massaged by a younger man—actually they were both under thirty.

"This is my associate," Jean said. He grimaced at me. "Mr. Missinge."

"Your *câfëè* is getting cold," the guy said pompously.

I took a sip. Meanwhile, Lafitte and the guy wrestled warmly in the precognition of friendship, each testing the resilience of the other's mental trampoline.

"What," Lafitte asked, or rather trapped Socratically, "do you suppose is the reason for America's lack of communism?"

The guy said: "The modern means of production, instead of coinciding with a stagnant surplus population, supply the relative deficiency of heads and hands—the feverishly youthful movement of material production. The New World hasn't yet the time or opportunity for abolishing the Old World spirit."

I took a room not far from the café, and copied every day from Jean's notes on Marx and Engels. We also followed our business interests closely. Most of Pierre's contacts were help-ful. True to form, Jean killed those that weren't.

Denise-Jeannette came one evening when I was alone. Stand-ing at the door holding a bulletin board, a pair of shorts, yellow sweatpants, and a T-shirt, she looked like someone whose entire world was in her arms.

"Do you mind if I come in?" she asked.

"Please," I said, disturbed by her beauty, "make yourself comfortable."

She rushed toward me and knocked me down. We kissed passionately and rolled on the hard floor. I put my hand under her skirt; her pussy was moist like a well-chewed cigar.

Thus it was that America did not interest me anymore.

goinG hOMe
To mothEr

When I tell you about my "mother," you'll just shit. Everyone in the world thinks she's such a holy fucking saint. She came to a little town near Acapulco—one of the many called San Opportune—and erased a small portion of the world's guilt. But no one asked me, What about your mother? The real one.

Grace took me to her home in Rome and became my "mother." Gave me my own apartment next door to hers and a governess who didn't call me her little wetback. Grace taught me English, bathed me in *pane e cioccolato* and herself in public glory. But she wouldn't let me touch her power source, her library, and I didn't, until I was twelve and old enough to lie. This sagging, disagreeable, jealous woman's library was surpassed in size only by her wardrobe. (Though not wholly unsympathetic: she clothed me as well as she did herself and let me be good-looking. With money and travel she was generous. But for the steady formation and development of my mental faculties, she had mostly jealous plans. This was a frustration I remember feeling well before I was ten, before I could even conceive of the real knowledge in her library; but although I couldn't count the number of volumes,

I fully felt their power. But I gave Grace more grief than she deserved.)

Grace had made art criticism the profession of stars—forget being an artist. Her book *Sucking Off Art* was a best-selling manifesto that established her preeminence before I was born. Her articles could and did make careers, or end them. Oh, the hate mail! Conflict of interest wasn't considered a flaw; she was hailed for honestly building up the careers of her lovers and wiping them out when another came along. A new form of art criticism. People said she only slept with the great ones, but let me tell you Henry Packshaw Henry, for instance, isn't half as great a painter as he is a pain in the ass.

In fact, none of her friends had the stamp of moral value—perhaps the truest test of an artist—and even as a youngster this nagged at me in the deep bowels of my intuition. I seemed to remember that my real mother had taught me better, and this may account in part for my persistent ambition to return to my real home.

One day I saw Grace do a strange thing. She carried one of her furs to the butcher. Odder still, the butcher gave her a leather satchel full of cash in exchange. It was the intricate leather satchel that held my interest at first.

Later she claimed the fur had been stolen. More cash from the insurance company.

My new governess was not a very scrupulous person either.

Tranquila had taken pictures of our more intimate moments to blackmail my "mother" with. Unfortunately, as I explained to her, "mother" gladly would have published the prints herself, in a frenzy of art criticism.

So we brought the butcher a fur on our own initiative and found him untouched or unconcerned by interfamily squabbles, neutrality being his accustomed position. Neither Tranquila nor I had enough imagination or experience to bargain effectively with him, but after all a fur is a fur.

I said good-bye to Tranquila at Leonardo da Vinci Airport on my fourteenth birthday. On my way across the Atlantic, I was so excited to be going home that I jerked off three times under my cotton blanket.

I had four heavy bags filled with presents for my real mother and the brothers and sisters I figured I had, clothes, magazines, condoms and other personal effects, a gold brooch I gave myself as a going away present, six hundred dollars in cash, and Tranquila's necklace as a reminder of that scarce emotion, sentiment.

Still ebullient, I got in a cab at Kennedy and ended up paying one hundred and eighty dollars on the meter to get to the Plaza—this was 1970, folks—plus I gave a fifty-dollar tip. So much for *sangfroid* and *savoir faire*. I walked into the lobby and ordered a suite.

"For how many?" the bellhop asked.

I spun around comically, looked over my shoulder, under my crotch, then said, "It looks like just you and me, babe."

"I'm sorry, young man, the hotel does not accept unaccompanied minors."

The world is a skin-deep place, and truly beautiful people are recognized and rewarded as such. By truly beautiful, I don't mean the 95 percent of the human race that has a cute nose or long legs, sexy eyes or hands or redeeming features, pleasant-looking and occasionally the love of a life, people who make a big hit at parties. I mean the one-in-a-million real beauties, people about whom there is no room for such a subjective thing as taste. They have the world coming in a completely different direction than it comes to the rest. People want to give to them, and that is a formidable, animal power. They learn to use that power without ever understanding that others don't have it. They learn to receive gifts and adulation, and how to let knowledge and business, money and *haute couture* (my current field), simply come to them.

There is an early time, however, when the power is there but the control is not, and the power can be used by anyone who comes into contact with it. So it was with me, a great-looking kid with all the world coming to him, maybe.

But this was nothing, a hotel clerk. "I am Grace ———'s son," I said. I was always ready to use "Mom's" name, and it often got me what I wanted. Sometimes more.

I had an open-ended ticket, and I decided to see New York before going home. Perhaps taking these couple of extra days was a sign of ambivalence.

My first visit was downtown, to the Figaro Café. Raoul, the owner, had been a painter and Grace's lover years ago, when we were last in New York. She bought him the café in exchange for his series of six cadmium-red canvases, each covered completely by a thin layer of Muenster cheese so that none of the red showed through. Cadmium is, of course, an expensive color, but it was worth it if you *knew* it was there.

I said hello. Since I was going to Mexico this week, he hoped I would come by in case he happened to have a little something for me to bring over there.

I went to the department stores and bought myself a suit. I went to a bar. I went to a club downtown and a bouncer checked my ID. The Last of the Red Hot Hippies.

A blonde appeared and said I was with her. This was enough for the bouncer and okay with me. Candy ushered me to a table and introduced me to her friends. I was partly disappointed, of course, since they were men, but I was curious as any outsider about the underground. For one thing, it was dark down there.

Barry, very tall and acne-scarred, boasted strangely: rock groups, writers, painters; Andy Warhol had been a personal friend; did I know "Bill" de Kooning—I did?!? I told him my name.

"Candy! That was your last chance!" He slapped the side of the table so violently that all the drinks spilled and fell off.

"But isn't he cute enough?" she sobbed, frightened suddenly. "Didn't you say to bring in some cute kid?"

"We can't use him! He's Grace ———'s kid."

"Well . . . then couldn't we kidnap him?" She looked at me apologetically. "I mean if it's okay with him."

"Tom!" Barry shouted. The bouncer came over. "She's through. She doesn't come back."

"Barry!"

"And get rid of this kid too. He's a minor."

"Barry! Please!"

The bouncer reached for her arm but she quickly kneed him in the balls. He took the table down with him, joining our drinks, which were obviously at the *avant-garde*. Barry pulled a comb out of his pocket, which handled correctly could fire one small-caliber bullet.

"Okay, I can take a hint," she huffed. I went out after her, but she hadn't waited for me. That was the end of the peace movement in New York City.

I spent two more days paying my respects to Western civilization. Then I had one hundred dollars left and decided to pay the hotel. I felt kind of bad knowing I wouldn't have any more dollars for Mexico. I wouldn't get to play great white missionary, I figured, and they were going to have to be happy to just have me.

The hotel bill caused me a fit of impotence and fury. I tore the sheets off the queen-size bed and rolled myself in them, crashing into the floor lamp and breaking one of the legs on the TV console.

I went back to the Figaro Café and told Raoul about my troubles. He was happy as hell to bail me out, and I didn't stop to ask him why. But he wasn't doing it for the simple joy of giving.

After I got my bags downtown, we had a little talk in the back of the café, which became my temporary home.

"Stick around a few days," he said, "and you can do me a favor"—which, he didn't have to remind me, I owed him— "you can take a package with you."

"A package of? Illegal?"

"My friend, at your age, nothing you do is illegal. Remember that."

This did not exonerate me from moral culpability, but that nicety is not what gave me pause. Fear was.

I got up to go, planning no return. "Okay," I said.

"Good. Sit down. Keep your trap shut. From now on you do only exactly what I say and nothing more or less."

I was assigned to the dishes, ostensibly because of my debt from the Plaza and because the dishes were piling up something awful. Raoul also set this muscular pygmy on me, and I couldn't eat lunch outside the kitchen without his company. I slept on a cot upstairs and m.p. slept in the same room so I couldn't sneak down the fire escape.

What was there to do but escalate the conflict?

"What are you, queer or something?" I smart-assed to m.p. He slapped my face and punched me in the gut. It took me half an hour to get my breathing normal again and three hours before I felt like wising off again.

"I bet you can't flex your brains as good as your arms."

Another smack, another move to my gut, but my knee was on its way up Candy-style, and m.p. was down brains first. I finished him off with a soup ladle to the medulla.

I took my bags and hailed a cab. The Waldorf-Astoria, thanks again to Grace.

I called Raoul the next morning, and he was very sweet. "Mike, I was worried for you. Where are you? Let me send someone to pick you up."

"No thanks. I just called to let you know I was still in town. I'll call back later, but in the meantime I've got some-

60

thing for you to work on. I'll want some money wired to an address in Mexico," I said, sounding the depths.

"No problem, just give me the where and the how much. It's as good as done."

"I trust you, Raoul."

"You should, Mike."

"I also believe in the Easter Bunny, Santa Claus, and the infallibility of the pope." I hung up.

I ordered breakfast and put away four eggs over-easy, six slices of toast, a pot of coffee, a glass of orange juice, and the three muffins in the basket. I would have ordered more, but I was too embarrassed at my appetite.

I went to Central Park and watched people neck on the rocks. I repelled the advances of a queer, watched little kids move in and around the kiddie zoo. Move like they've got no worries, they're not thinking about this or that, or about what their arms are doing. They run *vroom* in a crooked trajectory in and out of balance at the same time and then maybe collapse onto a pile of other collapsed kids. An unpremeditated and yet not completely spontaneous pile. Their lightness and laughter and the careless flailing of their arms moved me to think about myself, although I can't explain the connection as it happened in my head. But I thought that a lot can change in a person, that they can become conscious of themselves in a short space of time, lose their grace, and that a lot of good looks and promise can go down the tubes. Or that, worse, the wrong kind of promise could be fulfilled; personally speaking, I could become like "Mom" or Raoul, on top but scared of the ephemeral value of all that I have.

I found a Woolworth's on Madison Avenue and broke my last fifty for a ten-dollar knapsack. I went back to the hotel and called Raoul.

"What's next?" he asked.

"Next is I go alone, no nothing, no bull. Good-bye."

"Bye, Mike," he said.

It was that easy to say no, I thought. I packed everything I needed from the four valises into the one knapsack, put the knapsack into a Macy's shopping bag, and I was set to saunter out of the hotel like one more guest on a shopping spree. I hoped I was like a little kid, discovering how to fall and land and coil up.

I took another cab, to Kennedy, and it cost less than fifteen bucks, tip thrown in. Imagine my surprise at seeing m.p. at the check-in counter, surely on orders, and lusting for revenge.

The police seemed out of the question and m.p. hadn't seen me yet, so I wheeled around and back to the taxi line. I ordered dinner to be sent up at the Waldorf.

Suddenly I was a poor young wetback with less than twenty bucks and an inflated self-image. And how thrilled my mama would be to see her son, broke and bearing ridiculous gifts that probably wouldn't fit or have any value. After eleven years, her son would be back no better than he was to begin with and maybe more useless. And what was I going back for? A few hours of fiesta? Wet hugs from Mama and maybe a scowl or two from the others? Maybe a private, well-deserved speech from the head of the family on how could anyone be so stupid as to throw away the only opportunity to get out of San Opportune.

I called the desk and got the international operator. Three minutes later I was talking to my "mother," the famous Miss ———.

"I thought I'd never hear from you again, you little bastard."

"I'm in real trouble, Mom."

"I can imagine. You don't know the half of it."

"I'm sorry about the fur."

"No kidding? Well don't worry about me, Michael, you know I can take care of my interests. Tranquila, on the other hand . . ."

"Grace, I need your help."

"You're on your own."

"I used your name to get a suite at the Waldorf."

There was a low whistle and then silence. Finally, "You sure don't stint when it comes to your comfort. That's a good sign."

"I had to. I was broke."

"And you were going to bring home oodles and oodles of pesos?"

Hoping to elicit some motherly concern, I said, "Raoul is forcing me to deliver a package to Mexico."

"I told you being a wetback would get you in trouble. Good luck to you, Michael."

The line was dead. I was too late for innocence, too early for power.

I called Raoul back. "You're the boss," I said.

"Remember, Mike, you can't shit a shitter." He agreed to pay my bill again.

I emptied my knapsack back into a single valise, so I would look more ordinary going through customs. After delivering the package and stopping in at San Opportuno with my presents, I'd come back to New York and work regularly for Raoul. Maybe do something less lucrative and more legal after I turned of age.

I didn't indulge in any self-pity, sure that I'd learn to handle my beautiful self, and that I'd get my hands on some books like Grace's, and that things would eventually flow toward me. The way things ephemeral attract light. I knew I'd have the wrong friends for many years. I promised myself to pursue something other than revenge and notoriety.

Just as I was leaving the room the phone rang. It was Miss —————— with a change of heart, if I skipped the trip to Mexico and just came back to Italy. As I said earlier, Grace never deserved all the grief I gave her.

I told her to go to hell.

tHe LASt doNna

I used to have an unusually strong love for my sister Ruth, partly because I protected her when she was twenty-four and I was seven years old. She was married to a mulatto Haitian who thought beating her up was a good way to work off tension from a day of real-estating.

I have a vivid memory of one time in particular, because it was the one time I saw her try to get away, and it was the first time I tried to save her; it wasn't the last for me.

I was at her home being baby-sat when he came in and they started to fight. He slapped her—and the next thing I knew, she was out the door and he was first calling and then running after her. I looked for a likely place to crawl under, and happened to glance at the tin sheriff's star pinned to my breast. What the hell kind of sheriff am I? I thought, accusing myself.

They came back together, he carrying her from behind, she kicking the door open with her bare feet. I noticed that her foot was bleeding between her big toe and the next, where he had stepped his heel in. The color of the blood and the nail polish didn't match—it was Fire Engine Red—and maybe this detail has also helped perpetuate a strange predilection I have for older women's feet.

I told him I'd arrest him if he didn't leave my sister alone. He told me to butt out.

That's the way it stood until she left him, and then there were other messes she got into, and me trying to help. I've always gone for older women, maybe because there was something absent in my relationship with my sister, or maybe because there was too much.

"I'll give you anything, Michael," Ruth said, "except sex."

"Why not?" I asked.

"Because I'm your sister," she said.

But she should have been as astonished at her statement as at my follow-up.

That's long in the past. When I called Donna and told her to meet me at the station in White Plains, I hadn't planned on staying for long. I took some things for the weekend—in case it went that far—and went to Grand Central.

A week earlier, I was lying on the sofa with Donna. She was on her back, lightly caressing my ankle with her toes. She looked like she was going to tell me something unpleasant, which she didn't want me to take too hard.

She'd found another job and was moving to White Plains.

I took it damn hard and stopped listening altogether. I don't know why I felt it had to be the end, because White Plains is only an hour away from New York City by train. But Donna wasn't talking to a pinhead, and I knew she knew she didn't have to spell things out.

I remember lying there trying to hold on to the feeling of intimacy. How she used to put her stockings on in front of me. How cool I was when I was in her room. And then I thought there's no point in getting sentimental.

*   *   *

I always found it pretty easy to meet older women, although they didn't often sleep with me. Mostly, I met them in laundromats or even at the park with their little kids. My first lover was my eighth grade English teacher.

She was a young woman, but nine years older than me, and that was a lot. She was thin and had a naughty manner in class. What got me from the start were her high heels. Some days she wore a high-heeled pump with a small hole over the big toe. Her toenail had a classic shape, and you could spy one red oval surrounded by black leather shoe. Perfect!

Apart from that, she was ordinary, and flat-chested. Most fourteen-year-olds are idiots about that; most of my friends talked about Stephanie Bergen, and they probably dreamed about our physics teacher, too—only they were too chicken to admit it.

I stayed in school late one afternoon, and five minutes before I knew she'd want to leave I went to Mrs. Klein's room and started a complicated discussion about who remembers what topic in Tolkien's *Lord of the Rings*. Predictably, Mrs. Klein didn't want to stay longer than she had to and offered me a lift part of the way home so we could finish our talk.

In her car, I barely listened or spoke. It was an almost ecstatic ride as I watched her feet manipulate the pedals. She asked impatiently—perhaps it was the tenth time she'd asked already—"Michael, where can I drop you?"

She left me off at an underpass on Queens Boulevard near her access to the Long Island Expressway. Queens Boulevard was a wide boulevard with fast-food chains, an Elks lodge, and an AFL-CIO local. Alexi and I once went in to ask them if we could borrow their copy of the *Communist Manifesto*. The receptionist smiled and put down her book; we bolted out without waiting for an answer. We thought nothing was funnier than assaulting unsuspecting middle-class matrons.

I also went door-to-door with Alexi, selling bogus orders for hedgehogs. My pitch was that they're nice on the sofa and a handy conversation piece. Twenty-five dollars COD. I got one order.

Hunting for crazy snapshots, I once found a dead German shepherd under that bridge where Mrs. Klein dropped me off. I got Alexi to pose next to it; he was good. He lay on his back with his arms and legs straight up in the air. I called it *Two Dead Dogs.*

So much for childhood adventures.

Mrs. Klein must have been out of her mind. I said no one would be home and she believed me. How she could trust a kid my age is beyond me.

It was difficult the first time. I found I couldn't get hard, much less get off, without a toe in my mouth. I made the whole procedure complicated and gymnastic, and it wasn't worth all the effort. But what did I know?

The next time, Mrs. Klein seemed to know what I wanted.

"Take your pants off," she ordered.

She lifted her dress over her head and kept her bra, red panties, and pumps on.

"Is this what you want?"

"Yeah," I croaked.

She pointed her foot at me and said, "Lick it with the shoe on."

I licked the smooth red varnish on the big toe, and then the instep laced with thin blue veins. Then I took off her shoe.

"I know just what you want," she said, wiggling her toes just out of reach of my lips.

When the school year ended, there was a dance that all the teachers were invited to. Mrs. Klein came with her husband.

He was a short, broad redhead with freckles. I hated him instantly and kept away from her all night. I imagined that he beat her every night, and that I had to rescue her.

At home that night, I composed a poem in which I begged her to leave her husband and live with me. I never heard from her again.

The next year I was in high school, and I fell in love with the senior class president. Her father was the Italian ice magnate of Queens. I called her up and told her, "You don't know me, but my name is Michael, and I'd like to go out with you. Maybe you've seen me in the halls?"

"No," she said.

I went back to older women.

Again, I have to stress that most of them didn't sleep with me, and I could tell why. I had a lot of pimples, plus I was under eighteen, so they couldn't take me everywhere they wanted—like Studio 54, for instance.

You might ask, Well, then why would they want to be with you? Couldn't they play with someone their own age?

No, no, they couldn't. Have you ever bothered to consider the choices women have? If height were given out in the same proportion as brains, most men would be able to roller-skate under Dunkin Donut counter stools. I ask you, How could they pass me up?

Even when I didn't get to sleep with them, it was an even trade as far as I was concerned. I was a good listener, which was good for them, and I was a good listener because I loved to listen. I found out stuff it takes most people fifteen years to learn, if they learn it at all.

*   *   *

The first time I saw Donna Booziak I was with her older sister, Rosy, who had just moved into our building.

Rosy was thin and flat-chested and had very little going for her upstairs. But being the bundle of sexed-up nerves that I was, she was a hippie goddess.

In exchange for beers and conversation, I sandpapered her kitchen table until my knuckles were too raw to continue.

I say conversation. With someone like Rosy it was easy. She was probably almost twice my age.

With girls my own age, it was impossible. People say don't worry, it'll come naturally—but people usually say a pack of lies.

The one time I actually went on a date with a girl, it was raining. We talked about the pizza, homework, what teachers we hated in common, and then I walked her home. I wasn't even bright enough to walk under the same umbrella with her. No good-bye kiss, nothing. I didn't do that again.

But I was always a hit with older women. No one in my family likes anyone else, and that's always a good conversation starter. No one would believe that even half the stuff was true, so I have to water it down a little.

For instance, I never say my older brother is in jail for being a con artist (the truth). People would think I'm a liar. So I tell them he's in jail for murder, and they eat it right up.

I have a sister in California my dad threw out of the house because she cursed out my mother. I tell people he threw her out for hooking.

So you can see I don't have problems finding things to say. People say I'm mature for my age after they hear that stuff. What they really mean is that it's a miracle I'm not in some psycho ward downtown. They get the idea I've learned a lot or grown a lot in some ways because my life is interesting. But none of this stuff is happening to me as much as I wish it was. It's happening to them, my family. It only affects me subtly. It depresses me somewhat. I wouldn't dare tell any of my pals, which is why all these older women are perfect for me.

I didn't like Donna at first. Maybe because she was younger than her sister—probably around twenty-one, though I never found out for sure.

She came in wearing blue sunglasses and tripping her brains out. She had to get together with their parents in a few hours, so Rosy brought some coke out of a drawer to help get her straight. Donna was more over-and-out than anyone I'd ever seen.

The coke is how I found out Rosy already had a boyfriend—a coke dealer. That's when I decided to focus on Donna instead.

She moved in with Rosy that fall and went to Queens Community College, majoring in psych. I was really bowled over because she was so bright.

I remember those days as my coke and Joni Mitchell days, because that's all we ever did together. We spent a lot of time in threes. But that changed when Donna got her own place in Astoria.

Donna wore a lot of denim the days when we first met, but that was something else which also changed once she started working full-time. I thought it was a change for the better. But Donna had flexible values. They changed depending on the circumstances.

It turned out that Donna already had a boyfriend, too. But I didn't find out about him until I was already in love with her. The worst of it was he wasn't a hateable guy. His name was Larry, and he was in the merchant marines; he was away a lot.

Donna was working as a receptionist in a fashion designer's showroom. She told me everything they say about men in the fashion world is true—they're all gay.

She was frustrated, and I commiserated with her, but I found it depressing that as long as she was going to be unfaithful to Larry, she couldn't do that with me.

I stayed over at her apartment often, and that impressed my friends enough. My mother was cool about it. In fact, my mother kind of cheered me on. My father wasn't too happy, but he was helpless. He went along with anything my mother wanted, except if she wanted him to forgive her foulmouthed daughter.

One of those nights, Donna told me she wasn't ready to fuck me yet. I hung around anyhow, not because I was patient, but because I had nothing better cooking.

I had to put up with some incredible bullshit. One of the side effects of being the harmless, sensitive guy was that sometimes I almost didn't exist as a man at all.

As an example, I drag out Donna's friend Sherry. She always wore sandals and a muddy-red nail polish. But she was a royal pain in the ass.

One night she came over fairly late while Donna and I were smoking pot and listening to the Grateful Dead. I was pissed at the sudden intrusion, because Donna and I were on the sofa and you never know.

Sherry was all in a snit because of (who else) her boyfriend, who thankfully I never met. God knows what atrocities he had committed in the past, but this night he had gone beyond the pale!

For the next hour, they cursed and groaned—Sherry cried, and Donna with her out of sympathy, and they played this song by Gloria Gaynor, "I Will Survive," which is about a woman who won't take her ex-lover back after he left her, because he was a bastard, and she found out she didn't need him anyhow. That's all well and good, but they played it fifteen times, and sang along and danced around and cursed men and all their ways.

And here's the crucial thing—at one point Donna turned to me and said, "Don't worry, we're not mad at you, you don't really count."

Sherry eventually broke up with her boyfriend (temporarily), and Donna thought it might be a good idea if I went out with her. I told Donna I didn't care about Sherry at all but that I wouldn't mind sleeping with her. The only objection I had was that Donna might change her mind about me, but I'd be with Sherry, and Donna wouldn't want to fuck up her women's solidarity let's-never-fight-over-a-man-because-they're-not-worth-it thing. Donna told me not to worry about it.

Sherry turned out not to be interested in me, but she was a worthless pinhead, and it pissed me off like hell whenever she came up in conversation.

Meanwhile Donna was still desperate because Larry was away. She was even going out at night with her faggy friends from the designer showroom.

One fine Saturday night we met them at eleven-thirty at a disco called P.T. Barnum's Ringling Room. Donna warned me in advance that it was a mixed place, including a lot of drag queens who really looked like women. And we were on our own once inside the joint.

I had met Rudy before, but none of the other guys. All of them were thin, tall, and balding—Rudy most of all. I felt awkward in my best polyester shirt, which Rudy informed me was one season out of style.

Donna was wearing a red dress cut down deep, dazzlingly high red heels, and red toenail polish. I never remembered her looking so good. I hoped like hell the whole damn place was gay.

It wasn't, and she was off in a corner doing poppers with a curly-haired geek she eventually gave her phone number to. Though she didn't sleep with him that night, the idea of it was probably enough to keep her satisfied.

Too bad.

There were three floors to P.T.'s, so I decided to get lost. The third floor was really nothing more than a balcony from which you could watch naked trapeze artists hang on to each other at eye level. The second floor was where you could watch them from below, through the holes in the net. I wasn't used to drinking as much as I was and got plastered fairly quickly. As a result, I couldn't keep my head tilted to watch them for very long and wandered in search of a woman instead.

Somehow Rudy found me up there and must have watched me for a while. I'd been eyeing the most gorgeous woman I'd ever seen while nonchalantly supporting a Greek column with my shoulder. Rudy came up as I was answering a smile with one of my own, and said, "Isn't that the most heavenly queen?"

I looked up at him, and he nodded and smiled. To this day I'm not absolutely convinced, but I took his word for it. He cupped my ass with his hand and asked me to dance.

I declined.

"You'll never know till you try," he said.

He smiled again and went away. I thought he was kind and almost reconsidered.

I found Donna downstairs; she was as drunk as I was and the poppers had worn off, so she was tired, too. The curly-haired guy was nowhere in sight. Rudy and his friends decided to go to a male-only after-hours place, so Donna and I took a cab back to Astoria.

73

"Rudy said for you to call him if you ever change your mind," she said in the cab.

Donna told me she'd given her number to that guy, and I was really upset.

"What about Larry?" I cried.

"What about him? He's gone for three more months."

"But he'll be back," I said.

"People change a lot," Donna said. "He's probably changed. I've changed. We're not the same people anymore. We probably won't even like each other anymore."

It was drunken drivel and I knew it. But I was hurt anyhow. I felt it all referred to me obliquely, and I hadn't changed, that was for sure. I was still loyal. Her theory scared me because I didn't understand it; it was beyond my experience. I felt attacked and betrayed. I argued with her all the way back. About how love doesn't die, how people don't really change essentially—they just evolve. God knows why I argued, because this was the news I was waiting for. With Larry out of the way, I could move in as the permanent boyfriend.

Inside her apartment, she got the spare sheets out and plopped them on the sofa as usual. I was almost in tears; she was furious with me. She went into her room and closed the door.

"Donna, we've got to straighten this out," I said.

I couldn't bear the thought of going to sleep with her mad at me.

"Get away from my door," she said.

"Donna, please," I insisted.

She said, "Don't force yourself like this, Michael, goddamn it. I have the right to not argue in my own house. Get that through your head."

"At least say good night," I sobbed.

"Good night," she said through the closed door.

*   *   *

I set up my bedding, allowing the tears to roll, and then cried loudly; I wanted to force her to come out to me out of pity. But she must have fallen asleep instantly.

I woke up to the smell of coffee and nail-varnish remover in the morning.

The curly-haired guy didn't turn out to be anything important, but he was good in bed, she said. I always got the details from Donna. She was always into drooling, and any one who couldn't get into it was out. She liked to drool her drool into the guy's mouth, and have him drool it back—hers or his, it didn't matter. She liked the spit to ooze out from between their mouths while they kissed. She liked having her tits, legs, face, lubricated, she said, with a coat of spit.

Apparently, the curly-haired guy was a good drooler.

I envied him.

And then Donna moved away. Away from her gay showroom, away from New York, away from Astoria, and up to White Plains.

When I got off the train at White Plains, there wasn't any Donna at the station. Maybe she thought I was on the next train. Every time one pulled in, I figured Donna thought that was the one I was on, and she'd show up to pick me up. I was mad at her, but at the same time I knew that the second I'd see her, my anger would disappear. It's always that way with people I love. I'm so glad to see them finally that I forget they kept me waiting so damn long.

There wasn't any shade in the parking lot, which was where I was waiting. I lost patience and decided to find her place on my own. I went on foot, and it didn't matter because I was glad to feel sorry for myself.

Donna didn't get home till late in the evening, and when she did, she had a guy wearing a checkered shirt and cords in tow. He had well-cared-for shoulder-length hair and looked rich in a suburban way.

"Hell, Mike, I forgot," Donna said.

She said she was real happy to see me, but it had slipped her mind until late, and then she guessed I'd gone back to Queens. She even seemed a little miffed because I was being puppy doggish.

Shit, I thought, isn't that what she has me around for?

I couldn't stand it anymore. I let myself get halfheartedly invited for a cup of coffee. I could see this guy was nice enough but that he was also hot for me to leave. I took my time with the coffee and then hit Donna up for a loan. I knew I'd never see her again, and this was my way of telling her. She didn't have much cash, so the guy said he'd lend me some. That was fine. He lent me sixty just to make sure it was enough, and my only regret was that he probably wasn't going to make her pay it back.

I thought it'd be just the thing to do, to take a Greyhound bus as far as I could. When I found out that was exactly Poughkeepsie, I said to hell with that.

Sixty bucks was plenty enough dough for killing a weekend and a memory without having to live off cat food. Then I won ten bucks at a church festival craps game, and that helped, too.

I didn't think about a hell of a lot, which is one way of forgetting. I found a paper and checked to see how the Yankees were doing. I realized I hadn't paid any attention to them in years.

My parents were pretty worried, and they had the entire New York State police force out looking for me. I can just picture my father assuming the command post, shoving people left and right.

It wasn't until I was in the White Plains prowl car on my way to the police station, and was trying to decide what I was

going to tell my parents, that I even thought about Donna
again.

Things occur suddenly, but a lot happens first. One
minute you're in love, then you're not. People move on without the slightest hesitation.

SUMMER romaNCE

I went to the airport to meet my cousin, a French girl. I drove like a lunatic, spinning through Van Wyck traffic.

I'd met Anne six summers before, when she was twelve, a doll. I'm twenty-three. She was just—you know what we mean—just a friend. There had never been anything more between us. The rest of it we talked ourselves into.

Over the years, I wrote her plenty of letters and asked her for pictures. She sent lots, and at first they were posed and graceless, but she was still beautiful. Later, she went through a coy period, when the pictures stopped coming altogether, and then a flamboyant time, when she was almost naked.

She was getting into it, I think, though she may have been a little unstable. Anyway, I cut out my favorite parts and made a giant collage of them.

I had spent the last four months of my life campaigning for her to come over for the summer. My mom was lending me the car and I had saved enough money for a long trip. Her parents finally said okay.

Then I had to convince Anne of the idea.

Please come, I wrote. I love you. I love you. I wonder

could you send me a nude picture, you know, or one with just your tits naked at least. Please come.

It isn't a matter of getting what you want or not. Most people are used to living with what they don't get. It's a matter of what you tell yourself and of what you pretend. That's what I learned.

The plane was late. Then three charter flights landed at the same gate at once, including hers. But no Anne. I went through a couple of doors and hallways I wasn't supposed to and stopped in front of two cops wearing sunglasses.

"I'm waiting for my cousin," I explained, knowing it sounded like a lie and not being able to prove anything, either. "Do you think she might be in here?" I said.

"See the game last night?" asked the cop.

"Fell asleep," the other cop said.

A woman at the Air France counter took pity on my wretched face and went to check for me. "There's no girl that looks like that in there," she said.

Maybe she's a blonde now, or she got a little taller, or maybe she changed her name. I was almost crying.

Only my fundamental belief in my own worthiness prevented me from deliberately crashing my car against a Van Wyck Expressway guard rail.

There was no answer at her apartment, or at her grandparents', just unfathomable, depthless, intercontinental clickings on the telephone line.

I slept fitfully next to the phone. It rang constantly, except when I awoke.

"Didn't she tell you?"—shocked French voice in struggling English. "She cannot come. We found the results of some exams. She lied to us, you understand, so we couldn't let her leave. We can't reward lying, you understand."

Sure, I understood. I was of course a mature adult.

Poor child.

A week later, when she arrived at Kennedy, and she seemed—at least she could walk—okay, I could hardly notice the effects of her feeble suicide attempt.

"You must be warm," my mom said to her.

"I'm fine," Anne said. Her long-sleeved sweater hid her wrists. She was sweating like a drug addict with the bends.

She called her parents to tell them she was in New York.

"I won't say it," she said. "No. I'm not sorry," she said. "I'm not."

She hung up. She laughed. "They've cut off my allowance," she said.

I stood there with my hands slightly outstretched, like a seller at the flea market who had just placed a porcelain rocking chair on a narrow glass shelf.

For me! I thought, though I was embarrassed to think like that. For me! She almost killed herself for my sake!

There it was, though, the truth, and what girl wouldn't?

We were supposed to stop in Cairo, Kentucky, to visit my relative Paul. We picked up a hitchhiker in New Jersey.

"Come with me to Frisco instead," the hitchhiker said. "You can stay with me and my friends."

"We have to go," I said. "We're expected." And besides, the whole idea sounded dangerous to me. I figured I'd tell the hitcher to get lost.

"*You* don't have to go," she said, pulling at Anne's hair.

"Okay," Anne said, "I want to go to Frisco."

I sneezed. Be reasonable, I thought.

"Okay, but let's stop in Cairo along the way," I said.

"I don't want to stop in Cairo," Anne said.

Women get their orders from outer space.

"You can stop if you want. We'll go ourselves and you can meet us," the hitcher said.

Right. Hi, Paul. Anne is on her way to San Francisco with a lesbian hitchhiker we met on the Jersey Turnpike.

"Nah," I said, throwing caution to the wind.

We were sick of sleeping in the car, so I got us a motel room somewhere in Utah. The highway was breathtaking and all that crap.

I called Paul from a phone booth.

"We're in Utah," I said. "We missed Kentucky."

"You missed it? Do you honestly expect me to believe that you just missed it?"

"Sort of. We'll stop on our way back," I said.

When I returned to the room, Anne and the hitcher still had their clothes on, but they were lying on the bed, kissing and roaming.

I backpedaled out the door and went to the bar.

A guy made conversation for an hour, and I didn't understand a word. Then he went away.

A woman came in and announced, "What I wouldn't do for a real man."

There was no one else. I felt bold.

She said, "You're not a virgin, are you? I'm a lover, not a teacher. Last one I had, he blew chunks all over himself, if you'll excuse my French."

*   *   *

There was a DO NOT DISTURB sign on our door.

"I'm going for a walk," I announced through the door.

"Okay!" I heard the hitcher call back.

"Don't worry if I'm late," I said.

"Okay!" I heard the hitcher say.

"Maybe I'll sleep in the car," I said.

"Whatever," I heard the hitcher say.

The lady's house somewhere in Utah.

"Straight or on ice?"

"I thought that was my job." I laughed easily, like no virgin, taking the bottle from her hands. Our fingers grazed sexually.

Later.

"Pour me another," the woman hiccupped—brazenly, I guess.

"Maybe you shouldn't," I said, letting the flea-market antique dealer in me get the upper hand.

"Give me the fucking bottle."

I sneezed.

We slept side by side that night. That kind of thing happens to me a lot. I've gotten used to it. She scratched my foot with her toenail in her sleep. I woke up early.

"It's great waking up next to someone in the morning," she said.

Yeah.

*   *   *

I knocked on the door.

"G'way," I heard someone say.

The only thing open was the truck stop, and with none of the romantic brunch food eastern yuppies dream of. It was inedible. I tried refusing to pay, but I was threatened, so I paid.

I was still hungry.

The motel restaurant opened. Anne and the hitcher came down, showered, pert.

The hitcher insisted on paying the motel bill.

In Nevada, she said, "You should have joined us."

"I didn't know," I said.

She sighed wearily.

I cursed myself up and down for being so dumb. But how was I supposed to know?

"How about tonight?" I asked.

"Michael," the hitcher said dryly, with patience patience patience, "try to stop planning things five years at a time. Leave that to the Chinese."

Anne laughed. Of course.

"We may all be dead by tonight," the hitcher added.

After that, I drove with extreme caution.

I couldn't tell you where the house was. We stayed only three days. I never drove out for groceries and the people in the house talked about The Haight like it was in the next county, so all I'm sure about is we weren't there.

It was three stories, two bathrooms, a monster living room, and skayty-eight bedrooms.

They talked as if the sixties were still going on.

No.

They talked as if everything had just ended. As if there

were fresh scores to be settled. As if it still mattered who was right. As if apathy was still the major obstacle we were all talking about.

Nostalgic for when they were just starting to be nostalgic. Rubbing the sands of time in old wounds.

Hey, you people had your chance. You blew it. Fuck you. Move over. You had the right idea. But let me at it.

I was draped in the mantle of my own brilliant self-pity. Everyone else was sitting around smoking something. Anne sat on the couch with her hand in the hitcher's lap. This was all just a romantically typical American scene Anne had probably been dreaming about. Her parents had been right, I thought.

She sprang off the couch and stretched like a young animal.

They were passing around an old argument.

I left.

I'm better off when I'm alone, almost at ease with myself. I was alone in my room. Masturbating, but so what?

A girl simultaneously knocked and entered.

"Hi," I said, stopping, but making no other effort.

"Whatcha up to?" she asked, sitting on my bed.

"Nothing. You know. Jerking off."

We sort of laughed.

"I think you're cute," she said. "Kind of square, but cute."

"I feel square," I said.

"Maybe, like, we could make it sometime. You know, get it on."

"Why wait?" I wondered.

"Now isn't the time," she said. "I think your friend is kind of in trouble."

"Cousin," I said.

*   *   *

Anne was on the couch, the hitcher on one side and the house guru on the other. They seemed intense, helping, and calm. Anne especially seemed calm. Asleep, in fact.

They pushed a Styrofoam cup of coffee at her lips, tilted her head, forced open her lips, and poured.

She gagged.

They slapped her a little. Kind of too hard, I thought.

"Someone should call a doctor," I said.

"It's been done," the guru said firmly, like shut up.

Shut up. Shut the fuck up. Shut the fuck up. Shut up.

Her eyes opened and sort of rolled around in the sockets.

She spoke softly, pausing lifetimes. "I know. I know. It's okay. I'll be okay."

Then her eyes shut and we knew she would not be okay.

I could picture trying to explain on the phone to Paris. I thought they were vitamins.

The house guests were all very calm, except for the precision and violence of their slaps and the attempts to make her heart beat again.

Hit her again! I thought, watching.

Aside from the phone calls, it was easy to get over her. I mean, what can feel worse than that Sunday night when you know there's no way in the world you're handing your homework in on time? That's the truly awful thing. No one has the decency to tell you when you're ten, "Kid, it'll never feel any worse than this."

So I'm telling.

thE VioLeNT SociEty

It was at the Noctambule before it reopened under its new, current management. Every Wednesday night, they dimmed the lights at 1 a.m. and brought out Fanny Jackson, the fat black striptease artist.

I stress that she was an artist.

I looked across the room, the way you do when you know what's coming, to see who else was in the know.

There was nothing sexy about Miss Fanny. There wasn't supposed to be. It was humiliation. She undressed to the beat, but quickly, to get that part over with. Meanwhile, the over-the-hill crowd danced next to the disconnected jukebox. The waiter flexed his arms and crossed them.

Miss Fanny had a gift, plucking the one curiosity seeker out of his chair and stripping him naked, slowly and with malice. That night it was a girl; better still.

"Hey!" the girl bleated, but her idiot boyfriend just smiled, like at a magic show.

The helpless girl was alone under the spots.

"Like my big black tits, honey?" Miss Fanny husked into the mike, low voiced.

The crowd applauded, encouraging the girl. She smiled and nodded yes, she did like them.

"Then let's see yours!"

First the top. Then the rest. The girl was shivering under the spot, hands covering her pubic hair. The crowd had formed a buffer between the stage and her seated, uncertain, unsmiling boyfriend.

Thrilled, I bit deeply into my knuckle.

"No! No!" the girl screamed when Miss Fanny produced the dildo.

"Calm yourself, honey," Miss Fanny purred, and we laughed. Oh sure.

"You can't have *this!*" Miss Fanny exploded, laughing and rubbing the foot-long dong between her tits.

"Ah! Oh! Honey!" she exclaimed. "Look."

She bent at the knees and parted her massive thighs.

"Show us yours," Miss Fanny encouraged, saintly smiling. "Come on, don't be shy."

The girl backed away, toward the edge of the stage.

"Watch your step, honey," Miss Fanny warned.

As the girl looked over her shoulder, Miss Fanny took a quick step forward and pushed. The girl fell into a sea of helpful arms. And applause.

"Get the bird." I heard a voice.

They brought out a yellow-throated bird, as big as one of Miss Fanny's hands. The crowd hushed.

She slit the bird from beak to bowel, pulled out its stomach, and threw it at the first wave of well-wishers. They dove under the upheld bird and let the blood fall on their cheeks.

I hadn't known birds could hold so much.

I went into business with my brother. He was a lot older than me and, according to my parents, a bad influence. I never understood that either. Like polluted water?

My first night of apprenticeship, I was hidden in a hotel closet with my eye up against the keyhole. I could smell the bed from there, and I could see half the room.

My brother brought in this sixty-year-old lady. Later, he swore she wasn't that old, but I can assure you she was.

She laughed a lot, because of what my brother said and how he said it. He was at the same time gallant and coarse, but had a kind of self-mocking swagger, as if the whole act were a wink. It wasn't Johnny, but she was laughing. I didn't know how she could fall for him.

I could see his hairy asshole so clearly, I started pulling at my underwear.

"Sex me," she whined, "oh, sex me," and then she breathed out like a goat—"Eeeh—eeeh—eeeh."

"Not so fast," Johnny moaned, "you're making me come."

And she believed him. I swear.

His pants were crumpled around his ankles. I knew what his underwear looked like, so I wasn't surprised he wasn't wearing any. I took some notes.

Johnny and the lady both had on their platform shoes. That's another thing—he wore them for real, and he thought they were still cool!

Since Johnny was raking in a lot of money, he didn't make me pay rent. We shared a big room in a Jackson Heights flophouse.

When things weren't so good, we stole olives and peanut butter from the A&P across Northern Boulevard.

One other thing, not that I think it means anything. When he didn't have a girl over, we shared the bed. Otherwise, I slept on a blanket in a corner.

"Michael?" he mumbled. "Where the fuck did we end up last night?"

"Here," I said, turning over on my back.

"Didn't we get any girls?"

"Yeah. We fucked them in the redhead's car."

"I thought so. How you feel?"

"Okay."

"I think I got it again."

"Shit."

"Fuck."

"Shit."

When Johnny got the syph, we didn't have a lot of money.

Johnny copped a medical discharge from the U.S. Navy. It went like this:

NAVY SHRINK: You admit knowing what you did is wrong?

JOHNNY: I do.

My mother sent me a note warning me about Johnny. She sent it to our room, and she still figured he wouldn't read it.

The evil guy was slender and cultivated, and he wore a dandy diamond in a gaudy gold setting. I stared at the fork on the table and thought about sinking it in the soft spot between his eyes.

But Johnny said you can count on me, and I didn't want to let him down. I had a highly developed sense of responsibility. At least on a par with my flight instinct.

I didn't have to do anything I didn't feel comfortable doing. That was the deal. Of course, I couldn't lose the mark. So I had to do certain things, perhaps. Simple things, like be a wallflower, listen to hear if a certain combination of words were spoken, not even listen, just hear, just be a human tuning fork. I was told what the words were. I had to hear them.

Then there was the letter; it went like this:

Dear Mr. JABLONSKI,

As you know, we have been compiling the *Com-
pleate* JABLONSKY *Family Encyclopaedia* for several
years. It includes the different branches of the JAB-
LONSKI clan, the several waves of JABLONSKI American
Emigration, the various noble titles held by the JAB-
LONSKI name (and includes those that still do bear the
JABLONSKY emblem!).

We've asked our printer to reserve 500 copies for
libraries and specialized bookstores across the country.
To order your own copies at reduced prices, to ensure
that you have the *Compleate* JABLONSKI *Family Encyclopaedia* in your home, fill out the coupon below.

With me working now, and with Johnny's letter, we were
raking in the money. But we kept the room, anyway. I don't
think either one of us got a special thrill out of it. It was more
likely a precaution against bad times. We both faced toward
the middle of the bed.

I told Johnny I didn't think I could handle all of the details of
the job.

"Michael, you got to trust me," he said.

Johnny had been through a lot. The sixties. Platform
shoes. He must know, I thought.

The cultivated man and Johnny and I were walking east,
in full public view, in Greenwich Village. But a lot can happen, even in public, east. Which is what happened. Mr. Cultivated spins around and hits me with the back side of his
hand, precisely with that V-shaped, sharpened-for-just-this-
purpose diamond. A cut opens up that wouldn't close. I began
to bleed what they call profusely.

"Lay off my brother," Johnny said. "Please."

Cultivated said, "You want to take it for him, Johnny?"

"Okay," Johnny said.

I leaned against a car, pressing my sleeve against the cut. I didn't know that when they rub sugar in your cut, it doesn't heal so fast.

Johnny was ripped like a red pin-striped shirt. His earring was pulled out of his ear.

Meat, meat, meat.

I watched like it was funny. When Cultivated was gone, Johnny said, "Better me than you, right?"

Later that week, Johnny was booked for mail fraud.

I was sitting in the Noctambule one afternoon, and the new owners were busy tossing around new chairs and tables. I'd heard they'd been looking to get a good deal on the place— nobody wanted to see that kind of garbage anymore.

Beats me.

I would pay two-fifty for a beer any night Fanny Jackson is up.

Johnny got ten to twenty in the violent society.

aFfAir

We were holding hands. I tried slipping her the tongue, but it was no go.

I had a lot of romantic fantasies about my job back then—not so much fantasies as versions of my life which didn't happen to be the way things turned out.

Well, selling books for a very high-quality house was the way it had turned out. And the truth was, I was going to have to sell fifteen or twenty books this particular day, or I'd never make quota by the end of the month. (When I say "sell ten books" or "sell twenty books," you understand, these are orders, not individual books.)

Anyway, the girl said to me, "Can you just sit here all day? Don't you have a boss or something?"

"I'm pretty independent," I said. "I don't stand for it when anybody sticks his nose in my business. Even if it is a person which happens to have hierarchical superiority to myself." (People are generally so beset with personal failures that it's a pain in the ass bothering with them. Like my ex-wife, for instance.)

*   *   *

I got to Larsen's Bookstore. Some other salesman was just leaving. The guy gives me a smile like I might as well forget it, he just got all of the shelf space in the Western hemisphere.

The phone is ringing. But Paul Buyer (not his real name, you jerk) cannot answer it, of course, because he is on the other phone. I always wanted to pick up one of those phones and say, "Who's this, Doubleday? Well, fuck off, Doubleday!" But I suppose it would be considered unprofessional.

People are always getting themselves all worked up over body language and communication skills, but I don't see the point. People have always communicated, and that includes lying; like even dogs also have communicated for ages. Me, I think dog piss contains coded stories the dogs tell back and forth through the ages, like generation after dog generation, always laughing their dog laughter.

Anyway, Paul Buyer gets off the phone. (Paul Buyer has a large mole growing behind his ear, which he fingers with anxiety and irritation.)

"Paul," I say with smoothness and friendship overflowing.

"I can't, Michael. Not today."

"Paul, this is Scarsdale," I say, meaning I've come all this way. (Nobody has much freedom, and nobody has less than a salesman.)

"Okay," he sighs. "After lunch. But I can only take five or six at most, and no new writers this time."

I hate this shit. Not that I have a personal thing about writers, new or old. It's just that I hate this shit.

I have to eat lunch all by myself. I was hoping to get out of Scarsdale before 3 p.m., but only after getting Paul Buyer to take at least eleven books (orders, I told you!) off of my hands. But instead of going back to Larsen's right away, I asked for another cup of coffee.

"Hey, I'm in publishing," I say to the girl who is sitting next to me at the counter. She is one of your typical girls from a rich town, not a hell of a lot to do, and probably thinking about sex and clothes all of the time.

"I'm here promoting a book," I say, like she even asked me something. "It's a new kind of love story." (There is, of course, no such thing, okay, jerk?)

"Who wrote it?" she says.

"This is only his first book, but it's very sexy," I say.

"I probably never heard of him anyhow," she says.

I wanted to impress her with some inside appreciation, as if my life had turned out otherwise. "It's a new story, but it's really based on a very classic idea," I say.

She shrugs. "I don't read so much anyway," she says.

She puffs on an ebony holder into which she has jammed a cigarette at an awkward angle. Her jeans come down to the line just above her ankles. Black pumps with a short heel. It was obvious she could have made something of herself. She could have been a real sexpot.

"There's a guy," I say, "and some other guy, a kind of good-looking and evil guy, and then there is these two very beautiful women. The hero's not very handsome, but he's funny and charming. And he really likes one of the babes. But he's really in love with the other one. Like crazy, you know? So the two babes are almost exactly alike. Same build. Same tits. Same everything. Except one of them is a blonde and the other one is this raven-haired beaut, and dresses very sexy, and this is the one which the hero guy is in love with. The story starts with when the guy has a fight with the babe's father, who is this rich bastard. I mean, you know, the father is against it."

"This sounds like 'The Patty Duke Show,' " she says. "You know, the identical cousins."

(That's how it is when you tell stories to people out loud.

Like the old guys, the guys on top of naked mountains, a campfire at night, the Stone Age. People interrupted, then you went on. Sometimes, you leave stuff out on purpose, and you have to say, "Just wait a minute, I'm getting to that." Even if it isn't true. Even if you never will.)

I told her more about the two babes, the blonde and the other one, like about how they used to be friends because they were almost like twins.

"The evil guy is highly good-looking, and he has this way when he smokes. He sucks on his cigarette and he sticks one finger in his eye. Kind of like an intellectual, you know? What happens is he sees this very passionate scene with the sexy girl and the hero guy. So when he gets the chance, he tells her that the hero guy was a coward during the war, which is all lies, as anybody could tell. So this babe is just shit anyway, so she breaks up with the guy, and the guy gets really depressed and wants to win her back, only the dumb fuck doesn't know how."

"How come she couldn't tell they were lies?" this girl interrupts me again.

"This is the point," I say. "You keep trying to tell the guy, 'This one's just as beautiful, and she would be just the same as the other one if she colored her hair a different color.' But nobody really pays any attention to her, except when they need to get their car fixed."

(Ordinarily, you don't tell this much about a book if you want somebody to read it. But I didn't think she was going to buy it anyway.)

"Then, he realizes that this girl is very beautiful and that he really loves her all along."

I was getting to the end of the story, and I had a good moral lined up too.

"I don't know anybody that didn't break up eventually," the girl says, jerking the cigarette out of the holder and crushing it with her heel.

Then she says, "The seasons are changing." (Women feel that in their hearts. Not like men, who say these things just to kill time.)

Once you lose someone's fundamental confidence, like your wife and kids, you have done something intangible and irrevocable; then you might as well kill yourself. You say, "Love me again or I'll bash my fucking head in."

But we'll never be as sincere as when they say, "The seasons are changing."

"What's your name?" I asked her.

It was some kind of *L* name. But I immediately forgot. I have trouble with names. But I like *L* names.

There are signs all over town pointing to a tiny stream, little footpaths, no cars allowed. Like with most affluent communities, Scarsdale is very proud of simple accoutrements such as graveyards, Pilgrim churches, duck ponds, and two-hundred-year-old trees.

When she suggested a walk by the stream, I could only imagine one single outcome.

"You must find your job very exciting," (let's call her) Linda said.

"It's very challenging, and I have a lot of freedom," I said, the uttering of which hurt. (I have never experienced freedom from fear.)

I moved my lips to her face again, but she slipped away.

"I like it here," Linda said. "I come here a lot."

I wondered if she meant that in a romantic way, telling me the story of her life.

"What time is it?" she says.

"I have to get going," she says.

"I really have to," she says.

"I can drive you there," I say.

"Oh no," she says. "It would take too long."

"I don't mind," I say. "It isn't every day that I meet this beautiful a person. And what else is freedom for?"

Meanwhile I am thinking that, on the other hand, it would be great. I could see Paul Buyer and then I could pick her up again for dinner and a movie, and I could be back in New York in time for "Star Trek," unless of course the improbable happened.

But then I would have to tell her that I was really just selling books for a living.

The last time I was at the movies in one of these small towns, they showed a short before the feature film, and a middle-aged usherette climbed onstage and stripped down to her Playtex Cross Your Heart Bra and panties. I wish they still showed the newsreel stuff about World War II.

All this time we are in my car and I have insisted, for some reason that I cannot understand, that I will drive her to Yonkers and wait in the car while she sees Mr. Averton. I can't remember who Mr. Averton is in her life because she told me while I was thinking about laying her, so I can't ask again. Maybe it will come up again in the context, I am hoping.

My feelings for her are like a giant motor making a lot of noise. But there is no heat. You know the machine is working, but you don't know what it's for.

So I am out of Scarsdale early for once. But I will have to return in the morning, unless of course I spend the night in Scarsdale, which would be very convenient. I hate thinking this way, though, because it is opportunistic. People think like this in New York, which is, I am sure, why people are not happy there anymore.

I thought that Linda didn't know a lot about me, and I wanted for her to feel that I was a good and sensitive person.

"I should go home later to feed my dog," I lied.

She says, "There isn't anybody to look after him?"

I say, "Oh, sure there is. My neighbor has a set of keys, and if I call him, he just takes care of things."

"He just does that?" she says.

"Sure," I said.

"I really am attached to that dog," I say, "though sometimes I have trouble expressing my feelings. I have very sentimental feelings about that dog."

We have a wonderful dinner of some stuff, and then I drove her home.

It occurred to me, as she was telling me about Mr. Overton, one of my hands on the wheel and the other groping, that she was admitting that she had always remained faithful to her "boyfriend Ira."

Maybe I should have given her a chance.

I pulled over and turned off the engine instead. I guess she didn't know why. So she just watched me. I had been very polite and unthreatening. But that kind of stuff hadn't gotten me anywhere.

I pulled her head to my lips and kissed her. Then I pushed her head down to my crotch. She said "Hey!" which is very general and could be interpreted as simply surprise.

"Quit it," she said.

I kept pushing.

She had a strong neck. It was like a dog pulling on a leash. I didn't care if I had to break her fucking neck. Her nails lashed out like tiny extraterrestrials on my face, and my cheeks were the mysterious red rivers of Mars. Nothing seemed like me at all. I punched her one, a short, painful, ineffective blow right in the chops.

She managed to unhook her seat belt with her one free hand and open the door. She tumbled out of the car headfirst, doing some kind of a semi-handstand on the curb with half her body still horizontal in the car. I grabbed her feet and banged her ankles together before shoving her the rest of the way out.

At least now I won't have to tell her the truth about my job.

And that I have never sung with the boys.

And that I have never held a friend to comfort his grief.

And that I have never overheard someone say, "Michael is a real good guy."

The Profound Convictions of Michael Famous

It was the early seventies, and no one was paying attention. To anything. I was back in the shadows, cramped up, worried about knocking off the table lamp and making too much noise. Not great form for a baseball player, I thought. I shortened up on the bat and tensed my muscles. The guy came through the door. I stepped forward, banged my knee on a table, chopped the bat on the back of his neck, and he went down, wriggling. The damn job wasn't finished yet. I got a quick suck of breath and slammed the bat down again on the top of his head. He stopped his damn commotion, and I bashed him again, mush this time, grinding my teeth with disgust. The skull bones had cracked like dry frosting, and the wood pushed freely against the soft red and gray cushion of life. A small vessel spurted a long stream of blood like poison from a cobra's mouth.

The first time you kill somebody, it's like your first acid trip. There's this difference between you and anyone else who hasn't done it. You've had a vision. You feel like you can't even talk to them—the others. And you look back at yourself as if that was another person, an amiable and innocent idiot.

I sniffed my fingers, searching for that sweet tobacco smell. This wasn't the first, and I can't say killing someone had been a turning point in my life. It just confirmed a tendency. I didn't feel like I had to reevaluate myself or my fundamental principles. Murders are common enough. And I was still against capital punishment, for instance.

I wondered how he was experiencing the time dying, what it felt like for him, if he was getting the most out of it. If he was a socially well-conditioned American, he should have been. We were going through that "live for the moment" thing. We were all hearing how killers, kidnappers, bank robbers, political terrorists, and weathermen from a small town called Woodbe had prodded the USA into shallow, resentful, and scatterbrained introspection. The "establishment" waited for the adolescent fit to pass.

I sat in that room for a while, looking at the guy's body. I could have killed him differently. But Wolfsheim said to make it messy so it didn't look like a professional job. Not that we are professionals. It was just the means to very important ends. Wolfsheim said you don't learn anything in life by always being the good guy. "Sometimes you play the cop. Sometimes you play the robber," Wolfsheim said.

I wanted to save humanity.

The guy's blood was spreading into the spaces between the linoleum squares. Soon it would start dripping through the ceiling of the room below, the manager would be called, the police, etc. I would be gone, though, and they'd be looking for an older guy. . . .

A few people could tell I was a kid. Fast-food franchise managers. Little League coaches. Sometimes, a woman sensed an anomaly somewhere. "You look like an abused child." Like that was supposed to seduce me. In my sleep, my dreams were still a kid's. Awake, it was a question of control, hiding what I felt, and never feeling afraid. Anybody can be an adult.

Wolfsheim couldn't have been a more casual and indifferent acquaintance, a friend of my father's from the old country. I called him from a phone booth and left a message with his service.

It was hot fucking Florida and I was sick of it. Where I was living smelled like plastic from an exploded Band-Aid factory. Plus, the weather, the scene, everything was green, flat green, paint green, lawn green, lime green. The kind of green that shows why green was never meant to be a primary color.

Wolfsheim would call again when he needed me, and I could count on him to find me. I walked over to Brohamer Field to kill time. It was getting late afternoon, so they would be taking infield. They would remember me. I had been the best showcase they ever had at Brohamer's school. When the parents come to see the school, Brohamer asks them if they want to see a typical learning situation. They'd see me with one instructor (personalized instruction), getting a hundred ground balls and committing every error in the book, kicking them away, throwing them in the dirt, into right field, or into the group of parents if I was feeling particularly spunky. The instructor would work patiently with me, and suddenly I could do no wrong. I'd get so good no one could miss noticing the improvement. Baseball was the first thing at which I ever excelled. Saying I was super was putting it mildly. Brohamer wasn't into charity.

The parents all applauded, and I smiled shyly, like a kid, and if they asked me, I explained that I was from Weehawken, New Jersey, and that I was here for two weeks, but that time had gone by too quickly and I hoped to Jesus my parents were going to renew.

I don't know what the instructors thought about my age. But I don't think those guys paid any attention anyway.

*   *   *

Parents were put off by Brohamer. He was crass, and his idea of mature, polite conversation was an off-color joke to the fathers and a "pardon my French" to the ladies. But Brohamer was great with me, maybe more comfortable because I think he saw himself. I could field and I could hit, a switch-hitter, line drives mostly; now and again a burst of power. It doesn't sound like much unless you realize how much better that is than most NCAA players. Brohamer had played for six different major-league teams from '61 to '68, two of which almost won the pennant, and though he was never a full-time player, somebody always seemed to need him.

Brohamer saw me in the stands. "Hell, Mike," he said, "glad you're back."

"Just to say hello," I said.

I was hoping he'd tell me some stories while we were at it. He knew a lot of great baseball stories. Brohamer knew stories about all the great guys. Mantle, Greenberg, Mays. Just because you were a pro didn't mean you didn't love baseball.

He went back down and told everyone how much better they looked today. It wasn't a lie, because you couldn't help getting better if you did a hundred of everything a day and played two games a day and sometimes one under the lights.

It was still the sixties, 1971, and I was really just a kid. I had definite feelings about baseball and women and politics. I couldn't stand that baseball was supposed to be unhip, reactionary. Personally, I never got a better groove than from playing ball. They said, "Everybody has to do their own thing," but baseball did not apply.

I called up Voltaire in New York. Every time we spoke, it was like this call didn't cost five thousand dollars a second, and we might get off on any old topic. This was our way of keeping in touch—pretending I was still living around the corner. Of course, Voltaire still lived with his folks.

"Guy wanted to buy all my paintings from my mother," he said. "He said he'd take them off her hands, like they were cluttering up the place. I didn't say he couldn't have them. I said he'd have to talk to my brother. You know how that sounds."

We laughed, because Voltaire's brother was in jail.

Voltaire had been the only kid that didn't try to kick my ass.

"Get bent," they used to say to me. I didn't know what the hell that meant. As a kid, I was scared. I was scared by the furniture that stood out like yellow shadows in the shadows. I was scared of the voices I heard in the street after I was put to bed, kids out late, hoodlums. I used to be afraid murder would become legal; that my mother would die and my father would be put in charge. "Murder" was also a game we used to play on the hill next to the Grand Central Parkway. Somebody threw you the ball and you'd run around with it until someone else tackled you, then everybody would pile on top and you'd let go of the ball, or throw it to someone, and the chase would start all over again. I never knew what the object of the game was, just like I never knew what the hell "get bent" meant.

During New York summer nights, the air conditioner would blow, sounding like the fan in a car after the motor's been turned off. The windows were shut. Inside, it was cold. The sound of the air conditioner was the only sound, and I listened to its only-ness. It was the sound of the empty summer, and when a car passed under the window, its rolling noise was an interruption of the air conditioner's only sound, the legitimate noise of the night, the silence of the summer. Like standing under the El in Queens, Roosevelt Avenue, with no trains coming but just the sound of summer, the night, an inevitability, mystery, adulthood, me-ness, and always hanging on as long as possible before sleep carried me off again. Then it's one night in Florida, and in a window across the yard, I see a man and his father working in the kitchen. I'm afraid they'll turn out the light.

Two weeks every summer, we drove in my parents' Buick Special to upstate New York, to one of the resorts in the Catskills, Fleischman's, where old people from Europe reenacted summer romances, flirting, card games, adult stuff. On the way, along the side of the small country roads, which my mother preferred because of the trees, we always went on by the longhairs, the hitchhikers, the barefooted, and the ridiculous. We laughed in our conspiratorial smugness. Fuck, I wanted to be an adult like my parents. Not be scared all the time.

I used to be afraid that both my parents would be dead, or that I would be another person, or that I wouldn't exist at all, or that I would be me but in a much worse place, surrounded by worse people.

I was born. One revolution, one world war, six million Jews, twenty million Russians, the Japs, the Free French, and *voilà*, one messiah, one me. For years, I was afraid it would be all over before I got my chance.

Before I could speak, my father was tender with me and spoke to me in invented languages at night and carried me out, squint-eyed, into company.

Company was the European leftovers, very pink, very old people, exotic dishes with foreign names like smorgasbord and rollmops, old music on a thing called a phonograph. Then my father stopped being tender, but the instruction went on as before. I asked him what those big paintings were in the living room. "Those are by Ernst Furman," my father said, like that was supposed to mean something to me.

"He was a great man. He was the first man to study cockroaches," my mother said. She was getting the hang of this American trait, the love of superlatives and first-evers. And I don't think they could have stood for it if I regarded this Furman guy as anything but a genius.

"He was my guru," my father said solemnly.

People began to say that I was old for my age. This may have been because my father was so old for his age, or because he was going to die, or because it looked like that I had a mission in life.

But I think it was because of the radio. The Yankees used to broadcast on the all-talk radio station, and I used to listen to all the games. When they played on the West Coast, with nobody listening except me and three old guys in Wood-haven, Phil Rizzuto and Frank Messer would describe these mid-June ball games between two fourth-place teams and talk about the players and the wives and how tough it is to park in Manhattan and other stuff I don't remember because I didn't understand. For them it was just to make the time go by because there wasn't anybody listening at 1 a.m. except those three guys in Woodhaven—they didn't know I was there, too. After the game, there was the Long John Silver and Candy Jones show, and just like the ball game, it was as if time wasn't moving along, like it was still 1957. Candy Jones sounded like a hot vixen to me, but she was probably eighty-three years old. It didn't matter because it was the radio, and there was more of that adult innuendo, stuff you couldn't say outright over the airwaves. I listened hard, fast becoming an adult.

Vernon was probably the kind of danger I would have liked to steer away from. But I wasn't afraid of Vernon. He belonged to the candy store. He had been to the war, and now he was back. Maybe he was really dead and he didn't know it; people die sometimes, and then they're reborn without ever noticing the difference. Anyway, he would lead a squad of us in an organized crash from behind someone's bushes, yelling at the top of his lungs, "Bang! BANG!" Tall and skinny, he could jump over the bushes that we crashed through, scratching our faces. He looked scared and happy at the same time. He had nothing to do with 1968 or Love and Peace, nothing about what the country associates with the sixties. Big deal. Vernon disappeared a while after a little girl got raped in the neighborhood. I never saw him again. He probably died and was reborn all over again, again.

I had a bunch of older brothers and sisters. I never had anything to do with most of them.

Sue, the youngest before me, told me stories at night and bought me presents with her allowance money. She got herself kicked out of the house. She had the usual childbearing problems: wife beating, intellectual starvation, homesickness. She left her husband and settled in a small city upstate where she met Blake, another messiah-type guy. He was an albino, which gave him sort of a premonition that he was marked for a special destiny, and he had a slight limp from another deformity, and he had overdeveloped his upper body, especially his shoulders, so he looked like a monster with a hop. Plus, he had tiny eyes. Sue and him moved to the Village, squatting around in different buildings, making leather wallets and stringing beads together. Then they moved back to Queens, to a small dark apartment across the street from the playground. I split my time between Sue's place and Voltaire's. Voltaire gave me all my reading material: Vonnegut, Huxley, *Memoirs of Hadrian* by Marguerite Yourcenar, *Baseball's Unforgettables* by Mac Davis, my first porno books. We did our first acid trip together.

My sister was the only family I knew besides my parents and the old people that came over on Sundays. Actually, I couldn't give a fuck about her, but I always knew a good deed when I sniffed one. I felt committed to improving her and her man's lot in life. Even at that age. But as I told you, people had been saying I was older than my age.

I was ten years old.

I was anxious to start saving the world.

Sue said she and Blake were going to Florida and did I want to come along.

My father was dying of cancer, but pretty slowly. I didn't know how to react, and I didn't have any heros to emulate. I used to try being Bobby Murcer of the Yankees, or George McGovern, or Blake. But there was no one I wanted to be except me. And as for my dad, I just wished he'd do it and die.

Some nights I snuck out of my parents' apartment and left without locking the door. If someone broke in and killed them, tough. I'd bring my sister rolls of bills and wads of Valiums I'd stolen from my mother. I was popular in the dark apartment. What was in it for me was the feeling I was changing somebody's life—and the beautiful walks home at four in the morning, the night air slowly throwing back its covers. There was no movement in time, just a short breeze.

Sometimes at dinner, my parents would fight bitterly about nothing, and ten minutes later they'd be holding hands and making a disgusting kiss sound at each other. "You know," my mother would say, "these little arguments between myself and your father don't really mean anything. We always love each other."

What made it sickening was that it was true.

There were things my father did not want me to become (baseball player, owner of a candy store), and there were things he threatened me with becoming (street sweeper, supermarket clerk) if I didn't get good grades. My mother always said I could become anything I wanted. "We'll be happy as long as you're happy," she'd say. My father would knife cleanly and precisely through the boiled beef.

"I want to be a fireman," I'd say. "I want to help people."

"Ach!" he would say, throwing down his knife and fork.

I wished I had a real enemy, someone I could pour my load onto. Enemy, disturber of the peace, leech, usurper, traitor, criminal! I'll crush your skull with a baseball bat, and the world will applaud a deed well done. But I was scared, a runner, pumping like the fastest fucking human and no one could catch me. One afternoon, I took a carving knife and furiously cut up a set of plastic-covered kitchen chairs. Anger and sadness bring on more anger and more sadness, like a long snot or like a magician's trick of knotted handkerchiefs.

When he was starting to seriously die, they sent him to a famous hospital in White Plains, New York. My mother checked us into the Roger Smith Hotel and spent her time at his bedside, waiting.

I was free to fuck around.

I got tired of jumping around corners at chambermaids, so I dressed up in my sheep-lined denim coat and kicked around corners in the snowbound city of White Plains, name that inspired visions of cattle and giants and cowboys. I tossed gigantic boulders with my bare hands like they were just snowballs. I stamped out villages, took on angry village men, and withstood their arrows and spears, which were painful but harmless.

Naturally, I had a favorite lunch joint, a reconverted railroad car like they had before it became hip to eat at truck stops, back when we said "with it" instead of "fashionable." You could actually break your neck walking up the fucking makeshift wooden stairs, and guys who ate there had hands like T-bones, so you didn't want to start any trouble.

"The usual," I said at the counter.

So okay, Wolfsheim found me there. He had been visiting my father.

Wolfsheim motioned with his head that we should sit at a booth.

He talked about suicide, society, and the words of Sophocles. He talked about worldliness, loneliness, and seduction.

"Michael," he said, "I want to help you. I know you'd like to be beyond the grasp of those you consider inferior, beneath your dignity as a human being."

I made like I knew what he meant.

"Right now, you are like a single-celled animal," Wolfsheim said. "An underwater polyp whose whole life consists in clinging to an underwater rock, giving life to another underwater single life, and dying. You are unaware of time as a factor in your existence. Your life is clinging to a rock until your death comes as the natural order of things."

I thought he must be depressed.

"My father talks like that sometimes," I said. "But I have other ideas about my life."

"When did you think you might begin?" Wolfsheim said, touching a nerve. "Good grades in school, college, fidelity, good actions?"

"Good actions," I said.

"Every good action begins with a trivial betrayal."

I nodded.

"Your mother and father are fools. Your father especially. For one thing, he married your mother." Wolfsheim paused, maybe to measure the effect he was having on me. "When your father was in a camp in France, you know the famous camps, I was already in New York. You know why I was in New York and he was still in Europe? Confidence. Your father trusted his Christian friends in Germany. He wrote letters to me in New York. He would ask me to send five dollars, and I'd answer about my lady problems, which, believe me, at the time were quite immense."

I sat back in my chair and let the enlightenment continue.

"Think about Hitler!" Wolfsheim said. "Think about Schweitzer! Think about Neil Armstrong!"

And so on.

Later that day, an old cart lady told me the end of the world was coming. I got pretty excited. It was something I didn't want to miss. I waited all night, listening to my mother's dumb sob stories. Then I went to bed and tried to keep my eyes open. I didn't even know what the end of the world was supposed to look like. I kept my eyes on the window. I heard all kinds of booming noises. But it was just trucks. I woke up in the morning mad as hell because I had fallen asleep and because I thought White Plains could have been spared if the world had ended.

But on the radio there was just more talk.

The next week, I was checked at the front door of my elementary school. Like I was too old, you know? The teachers recognized me, but it was like I was an old student who had come back to visit. The only place I got business as usual was in the lunchroom, from the cheap bitch behind the ladle. I took this as some kind of sign, like the world was ready. I didn't know if it was Wolfsheim that had adulted me, or if I had figured it out all by myself. Now, I tend to spread the glory evenly between us. As I said earlier though, it was a matter of being in control. And not being scared.

When Voltaire spread his books out on the dining-room table, it was an occasion. His whole family of eighteen million people shut right the fuck up. Even the TV got turned off.

Some days we didn't go to school and played a kind of Monopoly game Voltaire had invented. You could buy Negroes and put them on your opponent's property to bring down its value, buy arson insurance. Or you could do the arson, you could murder people. Voltaire drew the board himself, made all the pieces, wrote the rules. I give it a lot of credit for the way I look at the world today. Indirectly, I mean. Voltaire said if we had more players, you could have betrayals and stuff. But we hated other people too much to ask them to play with us.

We got stopped by South Carolina state cops. All we had in the car was three thousand in stolen American Express checks and half a kilo of Tijuana red. The cops came along on either side of the car. One of them was holding his gun; the other had himself a pump-action. Before my sister could start shouting peace/hate slogans, I was out of the car and admiring the shotgun.

"Is it real, officer?" I asked.

Naturally, he took me for some kind of kid.

"See your licenseregistration," the other cop said to Blake.

Blake gave the cop his license. But Blake didn't have the registration. The car was stolen.

"Do you ever shoot people?" I asked.

"If I have to, little guy," the cop said.

"How many people you shot?" I said.

"Lester, get on the radio about the car," the other cop said, holstering his gun and smiling at me.

"We just borrowed it from a friend," my sister said. "He, you know, forgot to give us the papers."

The cop with the shotgun smiled at me and unhooked the radio.

"Can I hold your gun?" I said.

The cop smiled and looked at his partner, who shrugged.

So the cop handed me over the shotgun. "Take care now, it's loaded," he said.

It was a heavy sucker, and I hoped it wouldn't kick me on my ass. I put one shell into each of South Carolina's Finest, or whatever the fuck they called themselves. There was nobody in sight except those two dumb cunts, Blake and my sister.

We moved around carefully after that. When we got to Florida, Sue didn't want to have anything more to do with cars. She associated them with murder.

American Express was after Blake because of the traveler's checks, the police were still after him for the stolen car back in New York, and worst of all, he was fucking stupid. He was a lost cause at a time when causes were everything. He was lucky he was my sister's cause. My sister had been my cause. I was Wolfsheim's cause, so where did that leave them?

I called Voltaire because he was the only one I missed, and we spent an hour on the phone. He was already popular with girls. It made sense. He had hair on his chest, and some guy with a gallery on Fifty-seventh Street wanted to show his paintings along with this other painter from Europe.

My sister started to make like this phone call was going to cost an arm and a leg.

"Get screwed," I said to my sister.

"Don't get fucking conceited," she said.

Anybody had any brains, my sister called them conceited. It was just a matter of time, I guess.

Wolfsheim always knew where to find me. He caught up with me as I was walking out of a supermarket with two sacks of stolen groceries—olives, anchovies, pickles, all that stuff my sister loved.

"You know a man named Val," Wolfsheim said.

"The guy with the records?"

Wolfsheim nodded.

Val was big, with thick purple scars from a car crash across his wise-guy face. Whenever somebody called his house, he always said, "Just call me the Answer Man." But he was just another would-be messiah, a paperback idealist, dreaming about joining the underground, reading R. Crumb comics, and about how much people were full of shit.

Wolfsheim loaded me with instructions, most of which I did not understand the purpose of.

So Val was trussed up, and we had exactly four hours to listen to his alphabetized record collection. Blake was getting ready to shoot up; I told him to skip it. This is a problem with amateurs like me. Not knowing the proper time and place.

"I can handle myself," he snarled.

"Lay off, Blake," I said.

Val had been wanting to screw my sister in the most obvious way.

"Fuck you," Blake said, limping and pointing his finger at me.

"Fuck *you*," I said.

"Fuck you," he said, with even greater conviction. "Even if you are her brother."

He swung his clumsy, overdeveloped right arm; I turned my head to one side and his fist grazed my chin. He thought he'd hit me, but I just grinned. That was when I had the idea of bashing his head in with a baseball bat. This time, I pulled the gun instead.

Now he was cool again. "We have to pull together, man. I mean we're in this together," Blake said.

"I'm not trying to play with your mind," he said. "There's so much more than this cheap shit business. Look what it's doing to us. We shouldn't be doing this."

It was this kind of bullshit I couldn't stand for in the older generation. The peace and love routine. And those days, everybody had to have a friend who was a black dude. What the fuck is a dude?

We were listening to Cream (right after Clapton in the alphabet) when the four hours rolled around. Ding dong.

I gagged Val tight and cut the circulation in his wrists.

"Open the door," I ordered.

Three hoods came in, two of them carrying suitcases. The other one I pointed the gun at. He moved like he had something in the back of his mind, and I didn't like his face.

"There is good," I said. "Step over here." And shit like that.

"Don't forget the horse," Blake said.

"Shut the fuck up," I said.

Either you go by instinct, or you do what you're told.

I was two yards away from the guy with the face. Blam! The other two guys moved. I shot a couple of shells into the walls around them. To calm myself, because for some reason I was shaking, and to send a message.

Val whmmphed and hmmmfd. Blake took the suitcases and ran.

Anybody can kill. Even a souped-up eleven-year-old kid. For a moment the floor rocks under your feet and something sweeps by your face, like a whiff of rotten garbage you get on some ghetto street. Then it's over. Time hasn't even moved.

Outside, there was a Buick and a guy wearing a hat. Up ahead, I could see Blake running. I got in the car and got off wherever the hell it was Wolfsheim had said. From there, I was supposed to take a bus, but I walked. I didn't notice what time it was or how many miles I was walking. I was thinking, If I'm just a kid again, then I haven't done this yet. Like a draft deferment. Time was a gadget in the palm of my hand. I was the fastest human. And I wasn't going back. Kids I was afraid of, and even now, when a kid looks at me, I know he can see through me. But adults are easy to understand.

*   *   *

"What the hell you get us into?" my sister wanted to know.

She must have thought I was being conceited again.

I said, "You guys must really have the shits. I hope you didn't chuck the money."

"I'm not telling you where it is until you tell us what the fuck is going on," my sister said.

The money wasn't my problem, so I figured they could keep it. I won't pretend that I wasn't greedy, but I wasn't greedy for money.

"You're never going to see so much money again the rest of your lives," I said.

I took my baseball mitt and scrammed.

My sister called to me from the door, waving an envelope. "Who's going to pay your fucking phone bill, asshole?"

I thought to myself, take some time off, give some thought to your education. Read the classics, Beethoven, all that crap my parents thought was important. Remember not to drink out of the bottle. Wipe your mouth firmly with the napkin after eating. I couldn't help thinking about that stuff. And what about saving humanity? That's the way I showed up at Brohamer's, which is where I met Eileen.

I followed her to her apartment, which was on the second floor of a garden apartment at Englewood Gardens. I waited outside while she took a shower and slipped into something more comfortable.

She recognized me and opened the door.

"I was just going to roll a joint," she said.

I smiled and sat on the couch, sniffing my fingers.

There were pictures of her as a younger woman on one wall. A lot of them were taken someplace in the country, surrounded by animals and a little kid. For some reason, I figured the kid must be dead by now.

Her face had a thin scar across her lower lip, and some kind of a wound near one eye that narrowed it to a slit. A touch of meanness. Maybe from a fight with another girl. My dick moved around uncomfortably.

"I used to be into all those sixties things," she said from the kitchen. She carried in two cups of coffee. "Prostitution, drugs."

Naturally. But I'm open-minded.

I asked her who the kid was.

"That's my daughter," she said with a little bit of pride. "She lives with her daddy."

We went out for a swank dinner at a prefabricated Greek diner which comes from the same factory where they get the Greek diner menus and the twenty-year-old sexless cunts that bring you to your booth with their long red nails.

I ate a New York–cut sirloin with mashed and gravy. Eileen ordered oysters and swordfish stuffed with crabmeat and seven seafoods.

The TV was the only light on in the house. I tried to kiss her, but she said she didn't feel well from something she ate. I put my hand on her belly, like I could heal her. I honestly thought I could, which shows what happens when power goes to your head.

Then this fuck called plaintively from downstairs, "Eileen . . . Eileen. I gotta talk to you, Eileen."

"Christ," she whispered. "I told Vinny to get lost."

From the street: "Eileen, let me up I gotta talk to you."

What I don't need, I thought, is some Vinny.

"Eileen."

I wondered if she would have the heart to fuck me with him down there. Could she fuck in the clutch?

"Tell him there's no one home," she said, choking.

"Eileen, please, Eileen."

She jumped up and turned off the TV.

"I know you're in there. Eileeeeeeen."

We listened to him drag the garbage cans across the driveway. Then I heard the sound of someone climbing.

Eileen bolted into her bedroom, and I grabbed a broom.

The guy was wriggling in through the window. I held the broom like a spear, rocked back for momentum, and jabbed him in the gut. He made a noise like a woman and latched onto the windowsill. I gave another solid push. He hit the lawn, kicked over the garbage cans, which rolled off the grass, over the concrete, and then off the curb and into the street. I yelled out the window, "I'm the baby-sitter. You want to leave a message?"

I'm not kidding—I must have come eleven times. Not counting the first time, when she had barely put my cock in her mouth.

In the morning, she wanted to cuddle with me, and I felt like running again. I was that scared. But that happened often when I was just waking up. Sometimes it took me a while to remember who the hell I was. Just enough time to stare at my feet and sniff my fingers, look around at the bare walls.

It was the time of year when big-league clubs hold tryouts, so I had a talk with Brohamer.

"It depends on what you want," he said. "I sure as hell won't mind. Shoot, one more Brohamer graduate makes good, you know. But can you stand being second-rate?"

"Second-rate, my ass," I said.

But I didn't go pro. And I was worried about losing touch with the sense of my life.

Voltaire was into his rebellion period. "This age is decadent," he said. "No values. Kids just think about discos, sex, dope. Think about what the Emperor Hadrian said."

So I married Eileen. Brohamer was my best man because Voltaire couldn't get away from home.

As usual, there was nobody to root for. Nobody gave a damn, and nobody was even paying attention. Listen up you assholes, I felt like screaming. Fucking screaming. And not because my life was off the tracks. I may not have known where I was headed, but that didn't scare me. Not as long as I was an adult.

I liked the sex. I sent Eileen to night school because you never stop learning.

I went to work for a consumer group. Wolfsheim was still sending me money, so it wasn't for that. I figured it was just a small step from saving people seventy-five cents on their electricity bill to saving all of humanity.

I met them. I learned to sell them anything. I learned sincerity. Eileen talked about that a lot—sincerity, spontaneity. I said there's no such thing as being spontaneous, but that just made her angry. She didn't think about it. She reminded me of my sister, and that wasn't a good sign.

"Sometimes I think you'd be happy if I was just one big foot," she said. "So you could frig yourself between my toes."

That was true, so I tried to fuck her without even touching them. I couldn't get off though, without at least thinking about her feet. Feet and fights.

We were both out of the house a fuck of a lot.

I got in bed around one o'clock one night, naked and lonely.

The phone rang.

"I'm not coming home tonight," Eileen said. "I'm with a friend."

"What the fuck does that mean?" I said.

"It's over, Mike," she said.

I was surprised as hell. I sat cross-legged on the floor, sniffing my fingers.

I felt like crying off and on for a week, but I didn't really give a fuck.

Finally, Wolfsheim called.

*   *   *

I was next to Gristolm, a suave multimillionaire, CEO of a giant multinational corporation, in the shittiest dump in Tampa. That was the way they wanted it, and he was trying to explain that to Pierre Verges, the Frog president of the Latin American division of Scumbag America, A Worldwide Services Company. It was, he said, so the grunts in the smaller regional offices wouldn't get all bent out of shape.

Gristolm was way ahead of his time. He knew about budget cutbacks, shit like that. "The Japs are doing it," he said.

"Les Japonais le font," I translated. That was my cover.

"Qu'ils aillent se faire foutre!" went the Frog. He was heavy, with thick biceps jammed into his short-sleeved shirt. I didn't know which one I was going to have to kill yet, but that didn't stop me from hoping. I hoped Verges wasn't the guy I was supposed to kill, because of the biceps.

Gristolm asked if I needed to take a leak or something.

"A glass of water," I said.

Gristolm got off his skinny ass and poured me one.

The other guys in the room smiled, but I could tell they hated the fuck out of me. Nobody else had enough guts to talk to Gristolm man to man, but it was no big deal.

Most of the time, Verges listened with his eyes closed. One of his financial guys was showing off how the Latin division was keeping up with budgetary predictions and all that shit.

"Hold on," said this Australian guy sitting next to Gristolm. He got up and pointed to the chart and argued about whether this figure took into account some other shit the French guy was trying to cover up.

In general, they were like a bunch of kids doing an oral report on Shakespeare, and I didn't like them any better for it, believe me.

Gristolm went to take a leak for the fiftieth time. Verges

smiled at me and offered me one of the stale cookies the secretary had brought in on a tray with weak coffee and lumps of humid sugar. I shook my head no, and though I smiled back, I knew what side of the fence that put me on.

I wrote out a long telegram to Wolfsheim in my room at night.

"Can I come in, kid?" Gristolm asked.

"Sure."

"Let's have a drink." He went over to the fridge. "Nothing but fucking whores in the lobby," he said. "Just how old are you?"

"Twenty-eight," I said. Every week, I got a year or two older.

"I didn't think you were that young. I wanted to ask. You do Spanish too?"

I said yes because I wanted to be friendly.

"The Filipino bastard in Manila thinks he speaks English, but I don't understand jack shit of what he says."

I nodded. But one way or the other, Gristolm was leaving Tampa without me.

I didn't want it to be the Frog, but I didn't want it to be Gristolm either; he was just lonely is all.

I sucked him off that night, and not for love or money. He needed it. He didn't take it the wrong way, either.

"I'm not a faggot," he said later. "This just makes us a little bit closer. Like friends."

But this guy could have friends like No-Neck Williams could wear a choke collar. I picked up my message from Wolfsheim during lunch the next day, and I said to Gristolm maybe we could have a drink before going to Manila.

*   *   *

The last time I saw my sister, she was with her new cause, some idiot savant taxi driver from Lauderdale. She didn't even remember who the hell Blake was, so I figured I didn't need to get rid of her. I was exercising my own judgment, which Wolfsheim said I should do once in a while, and it was just as well, because killing a member of your own family is likely to stay with you. Blake could link me to South Carolina and all that other Florida business. Wolfsheim hinted that I needed to kill him, so I traced him to the motel before I went back to New York.

I needed to have a talk with Wolfsheim, because this killing business wasn't getting me anywhere, and maybe that was exactly his point.

[I I]

I went through a doorway in Queens, up a tight little staircase to a small office with a glass door, the kind that reveals nothing about what goes on.

"What the fuck do you do in this crummy office?" I said.

I wasn't just being a wise guy. There were three or four telephones, stacks of manila envelopes on the floor, a blueprint spread across his desk, another small desk with a typewriter and a secretary, filing cabinets. And a table with spools of film in metal canisters.

Wolfsheim asked me couldn't I see he was on the phone. He picked up one of the phones and dialed, then got into a long and screaming conversation. I figured he was getting senile. He had four curly hairs that were trying their best to hang on to the top of his head.

The doorbell rang, and Wolfsheim jumped. He left the receiver flat on the table and rustled some papers around.

When he found the gun, he nodded to the secretary, and she opened the door. It was the UPS man. Wolfsheim put the gun down, signed the receipt, and snatched the package like it was going to save his life one of these days.

He went back to his desk and slammed the receiver back on the cradle. "Son of a bitch," he said.

I asked him again.

"One of my interests is in journalism," Wolfsheim said. "I own interest in two newspapers in this city."

"What do you need two papers for?"

"The illusion of competition is a valuable commodity. But enough show-and-tell. I have another job for you—something terrible."

"Hold on," I said. "I've done everything you told me, including use my own judgment. You said I'd learn and I did. But I've done enough bad stuff. We had a deal. When do I get to start saving the world?"

"When you're old enough to wipe your own ass, you can do all the good you want to, but for now you work for me, and the only definition of good is what's good for me."

For a second, I considered walking out on him, abruptly, door-slammingly, but also I'd want him to run after me, begging. And I knew he wouldn't, and he might not even let me back.

"I don't want to kill people anymore," I said.

"This isn't that kind of job. It's a seduction, and I think you do that very well. And a betrayal. Seduction and betrayal. You won't kill her. You'll break her heart."

"Who is she?" I asked.

"An old lady I used to trust."

I imagined sagging tits, thickly veined thighs, the sour breath of real age, her valiant efforts, chipped nail polish, smudged pink lipstick.

*   *   *

I did some research on Charlotte Deluxe. Her husband had left her a fortune. He was still listed in some Who's Who, and there was a picture of her, even if it didn't do her justice. She lived in Cairo, New York, a mansion and a yacht.

"Sometimes you seem like a little baby. And sometimes you look like an old man. Your face," she said.

"Oh yeah?" I said.

"Don't misunderstand me. I love it, I think it's great. Innocent and wise."

"I have an older sister," I said. "She was an influence."

"I love you," she said.

"I love you," I said back.

She had just taken a shower. I sniffed the tobacco on my fingers and pushed her roughly on the bed. She had orange painted on her long toenails and it drove me crazy. I kissed her foot. She scratched my face with it, and I threw my weight into her. We made the sucking sound. I was above our bodies, softly bouncing off bookshelves, closets, dressers.

"Bew," she said, for *beautiful.*

"Do you want to take another shower?" I asked her.

"No. I want to keep your smell with me."

I called Voltaire from the hall telephone. I had nothing left to hide.

"Tell me about the Yankees."

"They all suck."

"What about Steve Klein?"

"He sucks too. I've decided. I'm going to paint full-time."

Catskill is a small town. It must have two or three different ways of getting out. But I got out alone and unnoticed.

The phone was already ringing when I stepped inside. Wolfsheim answered and then put his hand over the mouthpiece.

"It's for you."

I put down my bag and took the phone.

"We hear you're planning a run for the presidency. Any comment?"

"None," I said. "I don't know how these rumors get started."

"Are you leaning Democrat or Republican?"

"I have no definite plans at all," I said. "When I've decided something, I'll call a press conference."

"We'll give you coverage in exchange for a scoop."

I hung up.

"Good," Wolfsheim said. "We have this one more thing to do together, and then our work will be finished.

"The religious thing is very touchy," Wolfsheim said. "We don't want you coming off like a zealot. The idea is you don't even believe in organized religion. You're a deist is what you say. You know what that is?"

I nodded.

"Don't go around telling people that you're the messiah. Leave that to others."

The first posters came out that week. Across the top, in four inch letters, it asked "HEARD OF MICHAEL FAMOUS?" There was a picture of my face in the foreground. In the background there was a kind of countryside with factories, a couple of young lovers holding hands with a little kid. Underneath, in smaller letters, reassuring, the answer: "Of course you have."

Voltaire was still living at home. I was in New York a lot now, but I didn't want to risk being seen with him. If there was one thing hanging over my head, it was this age thing. No one was paying attention yet, but I was afraid it would come up sooner or later.

"Remember the sad," Voltaire said.

"How can you base policy on the sad?"

"Don't start sounding like one of them," he admonished. "I know you're going to do something different, no matter what you promise. But when you talk to me, drop the act."

It was hard to be Voltaire's, or anybody's, friend. I wanted to be left alone with my destiny.

"I appreciate your confidence," I said.

It was a thing I was used to saying too.

Wolfsheim called.

"I want you to make a speech in Omaha."

"What am I supposed to say?"

"Whatever you want. I have faith."

I was in a park, on a wooden platform. There were a few hundred Omahanians.

"We all have our dreams," I said. "I too have my dreams. I dream of America, of this great place, of this great potential for greatness."

They called it the Omaha speech.

On the phone, it was Wolfsheim.

"By the way, your father died. The funeral is the day after tomorrow."

It was a Jewish ceremony; no one in the family was supposed to carry the coffin or anything. My sister and my mother were there. All the women in the family were widowed, alone, for the asking.

My brother, one that I hadn't seen in sixteen million years, was crying his eyes out. It was a spectacular moment in his personal history. He threw himself on the ground, grabbed handfuls of earth, and started chucking them into the hole.

The old men from the synagogue grabbed him by both his arms and dragged him away. "Control yourself," one of them admonished.

"Daddy," he bawled.

I understood him. Funerals are a good place to get in touch with your own feelings. I was still young enough to know.

Later, Voltaire reached into his jacket and handed me a beat-up paperback, *Baseball's Unforgettables* by Mac Davis, published by Bantam Books. I kissed him on the cheek.

"What are you going to do now?" Voltaire said.

I told him.

"My name's Mike," I said.

"Hello," she said.

"You follow baseball?" I said.

"The Red Sox," she said.

I winked at the cap.

"I love the Yankees," she said.

I pulled her roughly to me and kissed her.

I kissed her again, because I was happy as hell to have found her.

"Bew," she said.

I daydream about getting *Baseball's Unforgettables* translated into French.

They don't get down on the fucking ball, their hands down and out front.

"Bring your bat closer, your hands, that's it. Now bend your knees. Remember, the hips first, swivel on your back leg, then your shoulders, arms, hands. Good."

They acted like they weren't paying attention, but they were.

"Hey," I said, "relax. You have all the time in the world."

A Note on the Type

This book was set in Caledonia, a Linotype face designed by
W. A. Dwiggins (1880-1956). It belongs to the family of
printing types called "modern face" by printers—a term used
to mark the change in style of type letters that occurred about
1800. Caledonia borders on the general design of Scotch
Roman, but is more freely drawn than that letter.

The titles were created on the Macintosh/Quark X Press.

Composed by American–Stratford Graphic Services, Inc.,
Brattleboro, Vermont
Printed and bound by Fairfield Graphics,
Fairfield, Pennsylvania
Designed by Irva Mandelbaum